Quinn took a s̶
turning her so
at her back wh̶

D0447386

He didn't go far, though, and kept his arms braced on either side of her. She looked up at him, and the expression on his face was so much better. Relaxed. Open. Happy.

I'm good for him.

That couldn't be right. They had chemistry, but they weren't a match, not for the long run.

She shouldn't have kissed him again. She shouldn't have let herself have another moment of pretending she belonged to him, of believing they had all the time in the world, when really, their time was up. She'd stolen a weekend with a man who wasn't meant for her, and now she had to pay for that theft.

* * *

THE DOCTORS MACDOWELL:
Doctors who have never taken time for love—until now!

Dear Reader,

The last MacDowell brother is about to meet his match. Quinn has reveled in his bachelor status while watching his brothers fall for their brides. He enjoys being one of Austin's hottest single doctors, but you know what they say: the bigger they are, the harder they fall.

As a cardiologist, Quinn deals with physics. Math. Predictable outcomes. I believe opposites attract, however, so Quinn really shouldn't be so surprised that a bubbly fun-seeker like Diana Connor is the one woman he finds irresistible despite himself.

Attraction is one thing, but building a love that will last with someone so different from yourself is another. Quinn and Diana cannot find their happily-ever-after unless they learn just what happiness is: a delightful accident, or a deliberate choice?

It's a question I found myself looking at from every angle as I wrote this book. I'd be very interested to know what you think. You can drop me a line through my website at www.carocarson.com, or we can meet on Facebook at www.facebook.com/AuthorCaroCarson.

If you enjoy the fictional world of West Central Texas Hospital, then you'll enjoy the story of Quinn's youngest brother in *Doctor, Soldier, Daddy,* and Quinn's oldest brother in *The Doctor's Former Fiancée.* Both books are available now—which brings up another good question. Don't you love it when you don't have to wait for the next book to come out? I hope you enjoy all three of The Doctors MacDowell.

Cheers,

Caro Carson

The Bachelor Doctor's Bride

Caro Carson

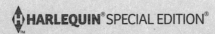

HARLEQUIN® SPECIAL EDITION®

Recycling programs
for this product may
not exist in your area.

ISBN-13: 978-0-373-65816-9

THE BACHELOR DOCTOR'S BRIDE

Copyright © 2014 by Caro Carson

Printed in U.S.A.

Books by Caro Carson

Harlequin Special Edition

Doctor, Soldier, Daddy #2286
The Doctor's Former Fiancée #2316
The Bachelor Doctor's Bride #2334

*The Doctors MacDowell

CARO CARSON

Despite a no-nonsense background as a West Point graduate and U.S. Army officer, Caro Carson has always treasured the happily-ever-after of a good romance novel. After reading romances no matter where in the world the army sent her, Caro began a career in the pharmaceutical industry. Little did she know the years she spent discussing science with physicians would provide excellent story material for her new career as a romance author. Now, Caro is delighted to be living her own happily-ever-after with her husband and two children in the great state of Florida, a location which has saved the coaster-loving, theme-park fanatic a fortune on plane tickets.

Dedication

For Katie and William, the two brightest lights in my life.

Acknowledgments

With many thanks to my family, who are getting very good at ignoring me when my headphones are in and I'm typing madly in my own little world.

And with gratitude for Kay Clark's quick reading and sharp eye, for T. Elliott Brown's savvy critiques, and for Catherine Kean, who casually stirred her tea one day and said two magical words that made my story fall into place: sock puppets.

Chapter One

A black-tie gala on a summer night ought to be the perfect setting for happiness. Glamour, romance, excitement—everything Diana Connor thought a person's life should have. So far, she was having a ball at this particular ball.

Downtown Austin's historic hotel, the Driskill, had pulled out all the stops, making the most out of its Victorian gilding by adding a crystal candelabra to the center of every table. Each one added prisms of real candlelight to the night. Diana couldn't remember the last time she'd seen real flames reflected through real crystal. Parties usually got their sparkle from plastic sequins and tiny LED lights—not that there was anything wrong with that. Diana enjoyed festive settings of any kind, but there was something extra special about tonight's real flames. Their movement echoed the dancing of the human glitterati on the dance floor.

The gala had attracted everyone who was anyone in central Texas, and the ballroom, the smaller parlor rooms, and the grand mezzanine were all part of the flow as everyone made their rounds, dancing and dining, seeing and being seen. All this glittering happiness benefited West Central Texas Hospital's new pediatric research project, making the evening a perfectly delightful way to raise money for a good cause.

Diana's boss hadn't thought so. The single thousand-dollar ticket he'd bought was the minimum he could donate to make his real estate company look marginally philanthropic. One after another, the top agents at the office had declined the use of the lone ticket to the hospital gala. When the ticket had made its way down to Diana, the ninth-best agent out of ten, she'd jumped at the chance to use it. Being solo was no problem; parties were meant for making new friends.

Her boss had given her gruff instructions with the ticket: *Give your business card to every doctor you meet, and tell them you sold that house to the MacDowells.* Diana had nodded politely, but she didn't waste precious space in her adorably tiny purse on business cards. If Lana and Braden MacDowell wanted to pass her name on to their friends, they would.

As it turned out, the MacDowells were here tonight—hardly a surprise, since they were both doctors at West Central. The surprise was that Diana knew them at all. Fate must have played a role when she'd first met Lana at a flower shop. Diana had spotted Lana, an eye-catching woman with jet-black hair, looking as harried as only a physician moving to Austin from out of state while starting a new job and planning a wedding could look.

Pretty darn harried.

Diana had offered to give Lana a second opinion on the bridal bouquets that seemed to be overwhelming her. When Lana had asked her if she knew a good DJ, too, Diana had been able to help, since dancing was her favorite thing to do on a Friday night. Lana had laughingly asked her if she could magically produce a dream home for her. Diana had been carrying her business cards that day. Fate was a wonderful thing.

Amazingly enough, helping a woman choose wedding flowers gave a person a good idea of what she might like in a house. Diana had found Lana and her husband their perfect home.

The MacDowells danced under the permanently blue sky painted on the ballroom's domed ceiling, a light and smiling couple in love. Later tonight, country-Western stars were going to entertain this high-paying crowd, but for now, the big band orchestra seemed like the right music for the MacDowells, a perfect match for them.

All around the chandeliered space, Diana saw good things. Laughing faces, liveliness, shimmer and shine. Everyone looked happy and satisfied. Everyone except…

Her gaze was drawn again to the one man who seemed utterly still in a room full of motion. His matte black tux drew the light in and kept it. He was supposed to reflect the light, didn't he know?

Champagne sips provided some discreet cover as Diana kept an eye on him, waiting for his date or his wife to return. The song ended, the dance floor cleared, and still, he brooded alone, sitting at an empty table near the dance floor while everyone else was mingling.

Diana frowned into her bubbly. She didn't like to see this man so unhappy. Then again, she didn't like to see anyone unhappy, and she was pretty good at cheering people up, so she and her champagne headed over.

It's going to be like cheering up James Bond.

Not a hardship, really. Handsome man in a tux?

I choose to accept this mission.

While she was grinning at her own silly thought, James Bond cut his gaze to her. Just, *bam.* One second he'd been brooding at the dance floor, the next, she'd been caught in a green-eyed, intense stare.

Oh, my.

She hadn't expected such sea-green eyes from a man with such richly brown hair. Handsome? Holy cow, handsome.

Those sea-green eyes stayed on her, but otherwise, the man didn't move a muscle. Handsome as all get-out, yes, but not happy at a happy party. She had a job to do.

"Hi," she said, while she was still a few feet away. The faintest lift of his brow revealed his surprise that she was headed for him. "Thanks for saving me a seat."

She gave the hem of her bright green dress a tug to be sure it wouldn't ride up and expose her derriere, then sat in the chair next to his. The dress was a little too short, but she'd fallen in love with its layers of fringe. Even when she moved only the tiniest bit, the fringe looked like she was dancing. Still, she was showing a lot more skin than usual. In an effort to look less like a '60s go-go girl and more like a flapper from the '20s, Diana had twisted her brownish—well, mostly red—hair into something resembling a short bob, secured with a jeweled brooch on the side. That had been another great reason to use her stingy boss's single ticket: the chance to play dress-up.

Oh, yes, it was a great ball. Time for James Bond to enjoy it, too.

First things first. She angled her chair toward his with a little scoot. She stuck her hand practically into his torso, so he had little choice but to shake it. "My name is Diana."

"Quinn," he said, then released her hand. His voice was somber. The poor man was serious from the inside out.

He glanced away from her, but she kept her gaze on him and saw muscles bunch a little as he clenched his jaw, quite a tense reaction to something. She followed his gaze. He was unhappy about…Lana MacDowell.

Uh-oh.

"I'm sorry to tell you," Diana said, "but she's married. Happily."

"Pardon?"

He said it like a cowboy, with just a touch of Texas twang, but the way he looked at her was purely upper-class offended dignity. He wore polished black cowboy boots with his tuxedo, as did probably half the men at this Austin ball, but he had "exclusive club" written all over him. Ivy League education, for certain.

Diana had to raise her voice as the music resumed. Who'd have guessed that a dozen people making up an orchestra could be as loud as any DJ with massive speakers? "She's married. Don't give her another thought."

"I wasn't," he said, without taking his eyes off Lana.

"Sure, you weren't."

Mr. Bond brooded on.

Diana sighed and sipped her champagne. "I hate to dash anyone's hopes, but that's one marriage that is going to last."

That got his attention. Those sea-green eyes looked directly at her again. Better at her than a married woman, she supposed.

"How do you know?" he asked.

"Lana and I are friends." For some reason, she added, "And business associates."

Business associates? It sounded like she was trying to say she was as accomplished as Dr. Lana MacDowell, but Diana was most definitely not med school material. Not Ivy League. Not even community college. Why did she want James Bond to think she was?

She wasn't his type. It was a simple fact. She could tell, at a glance, that this man would squarely put her in the buddy category. Maybe little sister—annoying little sister.

I'm not annoying, I'm friendly. Her heart was in the right place, so she wasn't worried if his initial impression was "annoying." She was going to be his buddy before the party was over, the gal pal who encouraged a guy to get out there and live. It was a role she fell into all the time. People liked her that way.

The poor man continued glowering as he watched Braden and Lana dance. "You're being a little too obvious," she said. "What is your name again?"

"Quinn." From his tone, she guessed he didn't like having to repeat himself.

Diana snapped her fingers. "Now I know who you are. I saw you on the hospital's bachelor calendar, didn't I?" She laughed out loud. "I didn't recognize you tonight with your clothes on."

"What?" He sounded baffled—or annoyed. Baffled was nicer, so she went with baffled.

"It's a joke. I've only seen you in your doctor duds,

the green scrubs. Didn't recognize you tonight with your real clothes on, get it?"

He didn't laugh, just sent a faint, polite smile in the direction of the dance floor. He probably preferred to get his humor from *The New Yorker*. Intellectual humor, not party joke humor.

Well, she was here to change all that. "Look, I'm good at matchmaking, so let's find someone else for you to think about. We need to salvage your evening."

That green gaze returned to her. "Do we? I wasn't aware I was so dangerously near rock bottom."

"You need to find the right woman for you. Lana isn't it."

He dropped his gaze, which meant he looked at her bare thighs being tickled by green fringe. Then he looked away, frowning faintly.

She tugged at her hem, relieved that he wasn't ogling her. She hated when guys mistook her friendliness as a sign that she wanted to party horizontally.

It was hard to imagine that anyone had persuaded this man to pose for a fund-raising man-candy calendar. Diana remembered the photo, though. He'd been glowering in that one, too, as if daring the camera to make him take his surgeon's garb off. She'd thought it was a shame the photographer hadn't succeeded.

"Lana and I are only friends," he said. "I'm well aware that she isn't available."

"And she never will be."

"The divorce rate among doctors is astronomical."

"The MacDowells are rock solid. Just put Lana out of your mind while we find you someone super special."

Despite the loud music, Diana could almost hear his snort of derision.

She pretended not to notice. Men often acted tough and grouchy when they were really sad and lonely. She'd rescued enough homeless dogs to recognize the gruff defense. "The good news is, you're far from a hopeless case. For starters, you're a man, so we don't have to work too hard to get you on the dance floor."

"I don't understand, Miss…?"

"Just call me Diana, please. 'Miss Connor' would be ridiculously stuffy."

"Miss Connor. What makes you think I'm in need of your matchmaking assistance?"

"Because you're sitting here sulking. Like a child."

Being blunt had the desired effect. The look on his face made her want to laugh. He couldn't even frown at her, she'd shocked him so greatly.

She nudged his shoulder with hers. "Don't take yourself so seriously—or me, either, for that matter. I'm friends with Lana, you're friends with Lana, so that makes us friends, too. As your friend, I'm here to help you get your party on."

He leaned back in his chair and crossed his arms over his chest. At least she had his attention—totally, this time—and he looked like he was actually close to smiling. "How fortunate for me. I thought I'd never manage to get my party on. It was worrying me considerably."

"Glad to hear we agree. Now, I was saying that you are at a big advantage because you're a man."

"Is that right?"

"You can ask a girl to dance. You have no idea what a luxury that is. This would be much harder if you were a woman. If you saw a likely candidate, you'd have to strategically stand where he could see you, make a little eye contact, flirt a little, and hope he asked you to dance."

"I doubt you are saying this from experience. You don't strike me as a wallflower."

"I never ask the man to dance. I only approached you because you were so obviously in need of a little coaching."

"Thank you."

"You'll thank me later, trust me," she said, answering his sarcasm with sauciness. "Now, what kind of woman do you think you want?"

He looked toward the dance floor, but Lana and Braden weren't there. They'd probably gotten a hotel room—they were practically on their honeymoon.

Diana sighed dramatically. "Okay, okay. You think Lana is the perfect woman. Then let's find you a woman like Lana." Diana scanned the crowd. "Gosh, everyone is so beautiful. The whole ballroom is beautiful. Isn't it great?"

When he made no comment, she turned to him. "Don't you think it's a great night?"

He shrugged, an uncaring movement of masculine shoulders under fine black wool.

"Well, it is. Everyone's so sparkly. And happy." She poked his lapel, earning herself another raised eyebrow. "And you're going to be happy tonight, too."

"What makes you think I'm not happy?"

Diana started to laugh, but she had the sudden intuition he was asking a sincere question. The man needed to take a good look in the mirror.

Diana decided to be that mirror. She crossed her arms over her chest and scowled, hard. Dropping her voice to the lowest bass she could manage, she said, "What makes you think I'm not happy?"

Quinn scowled back at her for a good, long while.

Then he uncrossed his arms and looked away with a little shake of his head. "That bad?"

"That bad, but not for long. Let me just find you the perfect partner."

"Do you often perform your matchmaking services for total strangers?"

"All the time." Every weekend, in fact, but she wasn't going to tell James Bond that. Every weekend, she volunteered at an animal shelter where she matched total strangers with the perfect pets.

This Quinn-in-a-tuxedo wouldn't appreciate that her skills had been honed on dogs, but people weren't much different. It was all a matter of finding complementing temperaments, something Diana had found success at by relying less on talking and more on facial expressions and body language.

Diana trusted her mad matchmaking skills. Lana would never have been right for Quinn, even if she'd been available, but Quinn would never believe Diana. Perhaps she should let him figure it out for himself. "Look—there's a Lana look-alike for you. Go ask her to dance."

When he didn't budge, she put her hand on his shoulder and pushed.

Quinn shook his head as he stood. "I can't believe I'm going to do this."

But he did. The woman was petite and slender, with shiny, straight black hair and an air of confidence about her. Diana watched her graciously present her hand to Quinn, so he could lead her to the dance floor. Like so many men in Texas, men who grew up leading women in the Texas two-step and country waltzes, Quinn was obviously a confident dancer. He and his partner looked elegant together, dancing to a Frank Sinatra standard.

Still, Diana wasn't surprised when Quinn returned after only one dance. The Lana-type wasn't what he needed.

"Well?" she prompted him as he sat next to her once more.

"She was the perfect woman—just ask her. She's chairing the board at whichever museum she said, and she's running a gardening gig, all out of the kindness of her heart."

"Charity work sounds like something Lana would do."

"She wouldn't brag about it."

"True, true. Your Lana look-alike was too old for you, anyway." Diana had a feeling this man would too easily retire into a sedate, settled lifestyle if she let him. Well, not if she herself let him, but if he were matched with the wrong woman, he'd find himself talking politics with gray-haired gentleman at a prestigious club in no time. Quinn was probably only thirty or so. He ought to be surfing or mountain-climbing, not serving on museum boards with a society wife.

"I'm afraid you're mistaken, my dear matchmaker," he said. "Lana's only two years older than I."

"She's taken. Get over it." Really, some cases needed a little tough love. Diana patted his arm, though, to soften her direct words. "Okay, at your three o'clock. Blonde in the sheath dress. A knock-out and still in her twenties. She might enjoy bungee jumping."

Suave Mr. Bond was apparently caught off guard by that. He gave away his surprise with a discreet cough, a polite clearing of the throat. "Is bungee jumping the criteria now?"

"Go."

Humoring her, which Diana took to be a sign of progress already, Quinn walked over and struck up a conversation. Diana watched his nod toward the dance floor, watched the woman light up and say yes. Who wouldn't?

It only lasted one dance. After a polite thank-you nod to the woman, Quinn returned to Diana.

"No?" she asked.

"No."

"Give me something to go on."

"She still lives at home with Daddy. Rich Daddy. She wanted to know if I thought a trip to Europe would really be more educational than a trip to the Caribbean. Daddy thinks it would be."

"Not Lana-like at all, you're right. You want someone more educated, then?"

"I want someone who is less into money. Lana's no gold digger."

Diana felt her first little zip of irritation toward him. She doubted he'd meant to insult her, but there it was. "I would never have matched you with a gold digger."

"I assure you, Daddy's Girl would be one very expensive entanglement."

From their side-by-side chairs, they could easily see the woman with her group of friends. She'd just dropped her gem-studded clutch. She made absolutely no move to pick it up, but pouted down at it, as if the purse had somehow misbehaved. Diana watched with amusement as another woman in her circle picked up the clutch and handed it back.

"That's not a gold digger, Quinn. She expects expensive things and an easy life, but only because she's always been given them. Always, from day one, and most definitely by Daddy. She just assumes everyone around her is rich, like she is. That's not the same thing as a gold digger. Those women calculate which man in the room has the most money and then go after him."

Quinn had started to take a breath to argue with her before she'd even finished her point, but to his credit, he stopped. Diana enjoyed one lovely, long moment of staring into his green, green eyes before they crinkled just a bit in what was precariously close to a smile.

"You're right. There is a difference. I stand corrected." He leaned close to Diana's ear and said, "But I'm still not interested."

His voice was warm. His tone was very assured, very in charge, but she could hear that touch of humor that lay just under the surface.

Diana felt...well, she felt antsy. There was something about Quinn that made her feel restless. The prospect of spending more time watching him dance with other women was not appealing. She needed to find a suitable partner for serious Quinn, and then she needed to get back to her mixing and her mingling.

That was all she'd come for tonight. Just a lovely, fun evening. She hadn't come to pass out business cards, and she certainly hadn't come to start brooding over a man who wouldn't stop brooding over Lana MacDowell.

The band struck up a song with a livelier beat. Diana stood, and when Quinn didn't follow, she grabbed his hand and practically hauled him out of his chair.

"Don't worry, Quinn, we're getting closer."

"I wasn't worried."

"Two o'clock, white dress. Guaranteed not to live at

home with Daddy. Looks like she's terribly educated, but still young enough to go bungee jumping with you."

"Haven't I danced with enough women?"

"Third time's the charm. She looks perfect for you."

Quinn looked toward the woman Diana had picked out. Diana studied his face, feeling some smug satisfaction as Quinn raised that eyebrow in reluctant approval. "Very well," he said, and he walked away.

Diana watched. Of course, the woman said hello graciously. Of course, the woman was soon smiling. Of course, the woman walked onto the dance floor and into Quinn's arms.

This time, Quinn looked like he was enjoying the conversation. His partner looked self-possessed and confident, which was excellent, because she wasn't going to be Quinn's girlfriend for long. Diana had just found him his rebound girl, the one who would help him get past this Lana phase.

The lady in white looked like she'd be able to handle it. She and Quinn would share some lovely evenings and mutual interests in the meantime, and then…

And then, when that phase was over and Lana was firmly out of Quinn's system, would he be open to a different kind of woman? One, say, with a love of parties and a passion for homeless pups?

Diana gave herself a mental shake. She was not a plotter and planner. She was the spontaneous girl who trusted her senses, and she'd sensed right away that this man needed a little fun in his life. That was what had drawn her to him, the desire to help a fellow human being enjoy life. Nothing more.

The woman he was dancing with was the one. Diana

could see it in everything about their body language. They looked right together.

Mission accomplished.

Diana toasted herself with a sip of her champagne. It still looked pretty in the glass, but it had grown warm and kind of flat.

She looked around the room, hoping to see someone with whom to strike up a conversation. It would be nice to enjoy herself with a man the way the woman in the white dress was enjoying herself with Quinn.

I'm the gal pal. Again.

Diana knew her role. There was always a character like her in movies and TV shows. Once the gal pal helped the guy decide to go for it, she exited, stage left.

Diana tapped her tiny purse against her thigh as she took one more look around at the crystal and the flames. They were pretty, but they didn't need her to continue brightening the night. Neither did Quinn.

Diana headed for the grand mezzanine. Maybe someone there was just waiting for a push in the right direction.

Chapter Two

Quinn MacDowell, M.D., was enjoying himself. His family would be surprised.

He was enjoying himself at a mandatory-attendance gala for the hospital. Forget his family's surprise; Quinn found himself somewhat astonished.

The reason he was enjoying himself was a bold and playful woman with hair the color of whiskey and a green dress that tantalized him with her every move. And that was—

Well, it was…

Unsettling.

At thirty-one years old, Quinn knew himself. He was a cardiologist. He dealt in physics, in measurable pressures and electrical impulses that powered the human body. He served on the board that governed the hospital his father had founded. He visited his mother on the homestead ranch, he badgered his brothers for getting married and tying themselves down, and he dated women who were polished, professional and career-oriented.

He knew himself.

If a complete stranger ordered him to dance with other women at a black-tie gala, then he, Quinn MacDowell, M.D., would never comply.

Never.

Yet here he was.

The woman in his arms purred her words in a cultured, educated voice. "It's so refreshing to have real music to dance to, not that auto-tuned nonsense, don't you think?"

She was stunningly beautiful. Every woman Diana had chosen for him had been so. As a matchmaker, Diana actually was good. Quinn had been exaggerating the flaws of his partners after each dance, but Diana had definitely picked out women in whom he'd normally be interested.

He'd fine-tuned his criteria over years of trial and error, and knew exactly the type of woman who fit into the lifestyle that his career as a cardiologist dictated. Long-term relationships saved time and effort when it came to dating, so Quinn generally dated a woman for a half-year or more. Eventually, the girlfriend would announce the need to move on, typically after reporting that her biological clock was ticking, or because she wanted to move into the ranks of the society matrons and needed to find someone with marriage in mind. With no hard feelings, they kissed goodbye.

His last kiss had been quite a while ago.

West Central Hospital had been floundering under

poor leadership, and it had taken all of Quinn's efforts to keep the ship afloat. Despite his aversion for corporate politics, he'd found himself incapable of standing by and watching his father's legacy flounder, so he'd joined the hospital board. There'd been very little time for female companionship this year, not while he'd been the only MacDowell still in town.

The hospital was going to survive. With some manipulation on Quinn's part, his oldest brother had left Manhattan to return to Austin, and a more competent CEO for West Central was hard to imagine. His brother's wife, Lana, the woman whom Diana claimed was her business associate, was rebuilding the research division. Quinn's youngest brother had finished his years of service in the army and now worked in the emergency department, and had just announced that he would take over as department chair in the fall.

All of which left Quinn with less of a professional burden to bear. He supposed the time was right for the next woman in his life. In fact, while he'd been watching Braden and Lana dance, he'd been thinking just that: something was missing in his life. Then Diana had appeared out of nowhere.

Now here he was, dancing with an entirely eligible woman, someone familiar to him as an acquaintance of an acquaintance. Tonight's rounds on the dance floor were tantamount to announcing that he was available, something that managed to get around his social circles with quiet efficiency. Appropriate women, like the one in his arms, would find him. Quinn would make a choice, and everything would proceed smoothly.

Diana Connor's matchmaking mission had been unnecessary.

Still, it was amazing, really, that a perfect stranger like Diana could take one glance at him, another glance around a crowded ballroom, and choose matches for him as well as he could have himself. By every measurable criterion, the woman Diana had chosen, the woman in white who was so smoothly following his lead on the dance floor, was perfect for him.

Yet, something wasn't quite right. He ought to be more interested in his dance partner. She pressed a little closer, causing her very well-supported, very expensively clad, very tastefully revealed cleavage to swell a bit against his chest.

He ought to be very interested, indeed.

But tonight, he was finding one thing utterly distracting: Diana herself. It was hard to focus on the woman in his arms when green fringe kept shimmying in his mind, shimmying its way over a curvy body that nearly crackled with energy.

To dance with her, to hold that woman in his arms, a woman so vibrant with her enthusiasm for life…

There was no hope for it. Diana had caught his attention completely, and no amount of cultured, educated, wealthy women that she threw his way could divert him.

Diana wasn't his type. He'd probably never run into her again after tonight. They didn't move in the same circles, despite her claim to be a business associate of his sister-in-law, Lana. After all, *he* was a business associate of Lana's. Diana did not work at West Central, that much Quinn knew.

There were other businesses besides medicine, of course, but there was nothing businesslike about Diana's behavior. She was too forward in her manner, too familiar in the way she spoke to a perfect stranger.

But she made him laugh. She poked and prodded him—literally—and he was certain that she had no idea that she was physically appealing in a way that was slowly sending him out of his mind. He'd spent the past half hour waiting for that green fringe to travel that last inch up her thighs.

Life had been all work and no play for too long. He was not going to let a curvaceous, vivacious woman with whiskey-colored hair slip through his fingers without a dance.

And if she refused to dance with him, but insisted he ask someone else of her choosing? Then Miss Diana Connor, the woman who seemed to think he had no idea how to pursue a woman, would find herself on the receiving end of all the charm Quinn MacDowell could muster.

He smiled.

The elegant woman in his arms thought it was meant for her.

Quinn changed directions in time to the music, a move designed to return his partner's focus to her feet rather than the smile on his face. He glanced toward the chairs he and Diana had been sharing.

She was gone.

"Strike three."

The deep voice caused Diana to stutter midstep. She whirled around, a quick pirouette in her smooth-soled sandals on the polished mezzanine floor. Quinn caught her elbow, stopping her so she squarely faced him. He stepped closer as he steadied her, so she found herself caught with just inches between a cold pillar at her back and a hot man at her front.

"Strike three?" she asked, leaning away from the pillar. Hot man in a tuxedo was infinitely preferable. Still, she was a bit baffled that he'd come to tell her his partner hadn't worked out. She'd left him with a woman who fit him perfectly.

What was more, Quinn didn't look very upset at striking out.

"What was the problem?" Diana asked.

"Let's go back to our seats." Quinn gestured toward the ballroom, and fell into place beside her. She half-expected him to offer her his arm in an old-fashioned way, but he didn't. Without touching, they walked side by side along the row of pillars. They'd definitely become buddies, just as she'd predicted.

Okay, Quinn, spill your guts to your gal pal.

Diana gave him the opening she knew he needed. "You can't tell me she wasn't educated enough. I could tell she was terribly educated just by looking at her."

"Terribly educated is right. She can't see why the Nobel committee overlooked the contributions of two scientists I've never heard of who discovered some molecular entity I've never heard of. And I'm a doctor, mind you."

Oh, he was most definitely a doctor. She knew this from the calendar, of course, but Quinn's career explained so much about him. Diana did not envy doctors. They were too often grim, too often facing long odds in their line of work. Someone had to do it, of course. Someone had to pit their skills against illness and injury, but Diana was glad to leave the life-and-death work to others.

Diana was satisfied with her matchmaking calling.

To bring in money, she matched people with homes. In her spare time, she matched people with dogs. And tonight, she'd taken it upon herself to match this doctor with a person who could help him lighten up.

"Here's the bright side, Quinn," she said, as she snagged a glass of champagne from one of the circulating waiters, "at least she knew how to say 'molecular entity.'"

That drew another smile from him. Diana was pleased that he'd stopped being stingy with the smiles. She was good at this, helping people enjoy themselves. In any group, Diana was the one who bubbled and chatted and smoothed over any awkwardness.

Sometimes, she wondered what would happen if she stopped. If she let herself have a bad day, if she groused at a neighbor or frowned at a stranger, was there another Diana out there who would try to cheer her up? If she wore a plain black dress and sat alone in a corner, would anyone notice she existed?

Diana never intended to find out. She'd continue making people happy, and they'd continue to include her in their world, the way Quinn was including her in his. One of her mother's best pieces of advice had been to follow the Scout philosophy of leaving the world a better place than you found it. Diana had taken that to heart, and always tried to leave people happier than she found them.

She returned his smile brightly. "We'll keep looking until we find the right one for you tonight."

Diana turned in a slow circle, eyeing the crowd over the rim of her champagne flute, gauging all the eligible women, taking in at a glance how they dressed, how they held themselves, how they smiled—or didn't. How they might match with Quinn.

"How about the girl in the red dress?"

"She's not very pretty. If we're going for someone like Lana, she'd have to be quite attractive."

"I'd tell you to get over the physical looks, but chemistry is everything. When you take the right woman in your arms tonight, you'll know. Since she'll be getting James Bond, it's only fair that she be a knockout, too."

"James Bond?"

"Ooh—I see a good one. At your six. Turn around casually."

"I haven't experienced this level of espionage since high school."

In his deadpan way, he was cracking jokes. Really, he was quite charming. Diana found herself laughing with him because she liked his sense of humor, no longer because she wanted him to follow her lead and lighten up. He was more of a serious person than she was, sure, but that gruff demeanor had softened into something more genuine. Maybe her mission had been accomplished despite his lack of a dancing partner.

Diana handed him her champagne flute. "Here, you need a drink after making small talk with strangers for the past three songs."

He took a sip. "It's warm."

"It's free. It's all included in this wonderful party. You've got to remember to look at the bright side of things."

The expression on his face changed just a tiny bit. Less critical, more thoughtful. "You're right, of course. Excuse me for a moment. Don't disappear." He left—with her champagne glass.

Diana entertained herself by awarding imaginary scores for the best gowns. When she spotted one young woman nervously tugging up her strapless dress and standing with her shoulders self-consciously stooped, Diana wanted to run over and hug her. It was obvious the young person had no idea just how pretty she was. If only Diana could tell her to throw her shoulders back and smile.

Diana had learned during her school years that she couldn't hug everyone. For one thing, it alarmed people, sometimes, to have strangers offer advice. She'd learned to approach people the way she approached new dogs, with a positive attitude and a hand outstretched in a nonthreatening way. She had yet to meet a dog that wouldn't be her friend, and humans were pretty much the same way.

Even people like her James Bond. Quinn seemed independent and self-sufficient, but Diana sensed that he was a lonely man. Subconsciously, he must know it, too. It was why he was accepting her help tonight, wasn't it?

The shy girl in the strapless gown that didn't quite fit would have to wait. Quinn was headed her way again, debonair in his black tuxedo, standing an inch taller than most of the men, moving easily through the sea of partygoers.

Look at the bright side. He's part of the party now, no longer standing alone.

He was part of the festive atmosphere, light reflecting off his dark hair as he nodded at acquaintances. He didn't stop walking to talk to anyone, however. He was heading directly back to her.

Diana twirled a piece of her fringe around one finger. Too bad they weren't each other's type. He was a damned good-looking guy.

"I'm sorry to have left you alone, but it was necessary

if you were going to insist that we drink champagne."
Quinn held up a bottle painted with flowers in one hand,
then set a pair of empty flutes down on the table nearest
them. He grabbed an unused napkin from a place setting and snapped it out of its elegant knot. With a twist,
he tucked it around the champagne bottle.

He had good hands.

"Were you a waiter?" she asked.

Quinn glanced up from his pouring.

Diana nodded toward the flutes. "You do this very
well."

And that simple compliment finally, finally, broke
through the last of Quinn's reserve. The suave smile
turned into something more.

He laughed.

Diana went still.

This is the man for me.

A man who laughed, a man who enjoyed life, now
that was the kind of man who could be a perfect match
for her, Ivy League or community college be damned.

If only he weren't on the rebound…if only he didn't
want a woman like Lana…a woman nothing like Diana.

Diana took the champagne he offered, glad for the excuse to get back in motion, grateful for the sharp bubbles
that woke up her taste buds. "It does taste better cold.
You were right."

He lifted his own glass to his lips with a grin, and
Diana felt her heart trip a little in the middle of its usually quick rhythm. He was lovesick over Lana MacDowell. She needed to remember that. The next woman he
dated would only be a phase, a transition to his next serious relationship.

Being this man's rebound girl would be crushing for someone like her. It was better to just be friends.

"I agree champagne is better cold," Quinn was saying, "but it's also better when it's actually champagne."

"I'm not sure what you mean."

"Champagne has to actually come from a part of France called 'Champagne.'"

The way he said it, all French-sounding with extra syllables, made her want to swoon. Diana had never swooned in her life, over anything. This man was positively dangerous.

"The waiters have been handing out some domestic swill. Sparkling wine, if you want to be kind."

"Oh." Diana glanced at the wrapped bottle.

"The effervescence in this champagne has more bite to it, but the fruit is smooth." He topped off her glass. "Try it again and tell me what you think."

What she thought? What she thought was that she was not in this man's league. She could see the beauty in the crystal and flames, but she could also enjoy the sequins and the LED lights. Quinn, she realized, was from a strictly crystal lifestyle.

They were not a match, no matter how much she was attracted to him.

For one thing, he was scoffing at the champagne at this beautiful party, something she would never do. It bothered her.

And so, for the first time that night—heck, for the first time in weeks—Diana frowned. She raised an eyebrow at him disapprovingly. "I think you can overdo the biting part. When someone offers you free champagne at a party, you should just relax and enjoy it, not critique it. Life is sweeter that way."

He raised an eyebrow right back at her—with ten times the withering effect that she could muster.

"Are you criticizing me for being critical?" he asked. Then, once more, he smiled. "I do believe there is a certain amount of irony there."

"No. Well…yes." Darn it, his smile was something dazzling. It was probably best if she moved on for the night. Diana looked around for the girl with the stooped shoulders.

"Miss Connor, would it be too critical of me to point out that you were just handed cold *and* free *and* genuine champagne?" He clinked his glass with hers, and sabotaged her resolve with another smile. "You are right. We have no choice but to relax and enjoy it."

Well. The man was obviously relaxed enough to start turning the charm on. If she directed him toward the right woman and he gave her that smile, Diana's mission would be accomplished. She took another sip. It really did taste special. She surreptitiously moved the napkin away from the bottle's label with one finger. One never knew when the name of a good champagne might be handy.

She took one more sip, and hoped she could fake some enthusiasm for finding Quinn someone to dance with. "All right, Quinn. Back to business. While we've got champagne, real champagne, to cover our movements, this is an easy time to check out the other people in the room. You never gave me your opinion on the knockout in the red dress."

Quinn took the champagne glass out of her hand and set it down methodically, precisely next to his. He looked rather stern. "I'm not interested."

"Don't give up. The night is still young. We'll find you someone worth dancing with."

"The bottom line is this, Diana Connor. The only woman I want to dance with, or talk to, or drink champagne with, is you."

"Me?"

Her heart skipped around in her chest, as crazy and out of sync as the fringe on her dress, shivering with the shaky breath she sucked in.

"You. May I have this dance?"

The orchestra began the opening strains of "Moonlight Serenade." It was all so perfect. The champagne, the man, the music, the night.

Diana felt a little shiver of fear. Dancing with Quinn seemed dangerous. Risky, somehow. What if life was never this perfect again?

It takes courage to be happy. Her mother's mantra had become her own. Diana had been doing her best to live a courageous life, seizing happiness when it came her way, just as she'd seized the ticket to this lovely gala. She could dance one perfect dance with a perfect man to a perfect song. It wouldn't change her life. It would be a happy memory to hold when the dark ones threatened.

"I love this song," she said to Quinn.

The corners of his eyes crinkled as his expression went from serious to something softer. Then a woman's voice called to him from behind Diana. "There you are, Quinn MacDowell. I thought for sure you would have ducked out by now. Being quite the trouper tonight, are you?"

Quinn's gaze flicked to someone beyond Diana's shoulder. Diana turned to see who was speaking. A woman, tall and confident, stepped in to kiss Quinn on the cheek.

Two facts warred for attention in Diana's mind. One, this woman could be a good match for Quinn. She was only a few inches taller than Diana, but her hair had been professionally and intricately piled on top of her head in a striking style that made her seem positively statuesque—and very confident. She wore a floor-length gown, one spectacular drape of blue cloth with a high, choker-style collar, a design only a woman with an elegant, long neck could wear.

Diana was not that woman.

Her second thought was more upsetting: Quinn's last name was MacDowell.

MacDowell. He's a MacDowell. He can't be in love with Lana. That would be horrible, in love with your relative's wife. Just horrible for him.

It was nearly enough to make Diana happy that the woman in blue would be a good match.

The woman trailed an entourage behind her, women who seemed lost in her wake. One was much older, dressed in a severe jacket over a floor-length, straight skirt, and one was much younger—the girl with the stooped shoulders. Diana smiled at her and nodded encouragingly.

The woman in blue, done kissing Quinn, set her purse on the table next to Diana's, and seemed ready to settle in for a chat. Diana took a step to the side to give her room, and felt the brush of the tablecloth against her bare leg.

Bare legs. She was completely underdressed for this event, something she'd noticed as soon as she'd arrived, but something she'd dismissed as being no more than an "oops." Next to this elegant friend of Quinn's, however, she wished for just a second that she'd worn a long gown. Too bad she didn't own a long gown. Formal balls weren't her usual Friday night.

"Thank God you're still here," the woman said to Quinn. "There isn't anyone worth talking to. Dance with me."

Quinn did the raised-eyebrow thing to her, but without any real animosity. The pair were obviously old friends. "As charmingly worded as that invitation was, I've asked Diana to dance."

Quinn nodded her way, and suddenly, Diana was the focus of attention. "Diana, this is Patricia Cargill."

Patricia looked her up and down, once, lingering for a millisecond on Diana's hemline.

Yes, I know everyone else is in a gown.

Quinn continued his introductions. "And, Patricia, this is Diana Connor. She's a friend of Lana's."

"A friend of Lana's." Patricia seemed mildly surprised at this. "From med school?"

Diana fought not to blush. This portion of her evening was rapidly coming to a close. His friends had found him; Quinn no longer needed her. Not even as a dance partner to wile away a song or two.

"I was Lana's real estate agent." She dared a quick glance at Quinn, then looked down to the tablecloth and her nearly empty champagne glass. There was nothing wrong with being a real estate agent, of course, but when she'd met Quinn, she'd said she was Lana's business associate. Had he thought she was a business associate from the world of medicine? Had he assumed she was a doctor or nurse when he'd asked her to dance?

Regardless, he surely had not assumed she paid her bills from the sale of Lana's house.

"Moonlight Serenade" was in full swing without her.

Diana stifled a sigh and turned to the other two women. She stuck her hand out so the stooped-shoulder girl would have to take it.

"My name is Diana. Isn't this a great ball?"

Chapter Three

Quinn kept one eye on Diana as she led the quiet girl into the ballroom's far corner. The other woman with Patricia had been introduced as Karen Weaver, the new director of the Austin-area's branch of Texas Rescue and Relief. Quinn kept Diana in his peripheral vision while he greeted Karen and said all the appropriate things about Texas Rescue's importance in times of crisis. He almost wished Diana could hear him, so she'd know he wasn't always as curt as he'd been when she'd first spoken to him. He had the requisite social graces. His mother had raised him right.

Karen Weaver said all the right things in return, complimenting Patricia on the quality of volunteers she recruited for Texas Rescue, physicians like Quinn.

Quinn had long volunteered with Texas Rescue and Relief, a home state organization that stood ready to offer medical help should natural disaster strike anywhere in Texas. Last summer, they'd sweltered in makeshift tents near the border of Oklahoma in order to provide medical care after tornados had torn through a small town.

"Yes, of course I'm committed to another year of service," Quinn assured the new director. "Let's hope the summer is hot, dry and boring."

He made a toasting gesture with his champagne flute, and Patricia tugged at his sleeve. "Do get me some champagne, would you?"

Quinn flagged a passing waiter to stop. Patricia took a flute as Karen declined, their momentary fuss giving Quinn the opportunity to focus on Diana. She was practically hiding behind a potted palm with the new girl.

"Who is the young lady you're dragging along?" he asked Patricia.

"My father's second wife's stepdaughter, or some such nonsense. I refuse to introduce her as a Cargill. She goes by the ironically perky name Becky." She hadn't taken a sip of her glass, but instead dumped the sparkling wine into the empty flute that sat on the table. Diana's empty flute.

"I thought your father was on his third wife now," Quinn said, sliding Diana's now-full flute closer to himself. "And this glass was in use, by the way."

Patricia shrugged. "I sincerely doubt your real estate agent will care what it was refilled with. And wife number three is exactly why I had no idea I'd be forced to babysit number two's offspring." She held her glass in front of Quinn. "Do pour a girl something halfway decent."

Quinn could hardly refuse her, although he'd planned

on putting that bottle to better use. He filled her glass. "You make a terrible wingman."

"Do I?" Patricia laughed. "Don't tell me Dr. Quinn MacDowell of the West Central MacDowells needs help landing a real estate agent for the evening, especially one dressed so... Or are you Cowboy Quinn of the River Mack Ranch tonight?"

Quinn hadn't tried to flaunt either side of himself, actually. Diana had talked to him as a complete stranger, without introduction. It was, he realized, unusual. Refreshing. Perfect strangers were perfect equals.

"Either way, she's not your type." Patricia slipped her arm through his.

"I'm in a better position than you to know my type." Quinn said it mildly. He included Karen in their conversation. "Don't worry. Your recruiter and I are not having a lover's spat. Patricia is merely the annoying sister I never had."

Still, being told Diana wasn't his type didn't sit well with him. Having an identifiable type seemed uninspiring. Monotonous. Was he required to stay within this restricted social circle of the hospital, Texas Rescue, and the ranch owner associations?

Haven't I dated all the available women in that pool?

They were all starting to blur together in his memory. It hadn't been hard to stay unattached this past year.

Tonight, he was suddenly obsessing about his own love life. It was ludicrous, when the only reason he'd attended this ball was specifically to fulfill his duties to the hospital as a board member. Meeting the new director of Texas Rescue was an efficient use of the evening, as well. Worrying about female companionship? Not on the radar. Not an issue. Not important.

He resisted the urge to look toward Diana's corner of the ballroom.

"Have you seen Marcel around?" Patricia asked, referring to her current escort. "He's so easy to lose. Oh, Lord—your redhead and my ex-step-in-law are on their way back. I can't take it. Quick, top off my glass."

Quinn only raised an eyebrow at her. To refill her glass would imply that he agreed that Patricia's gloomy girl and the bubbly Diana were burdens best borne with the help of alcohol. Quinn didn't know the girl, of course, but Diana's company didn't require a dose of alcohol. She was not a part of their usual circle, but being with her was no burden.

Diana emerged from the corner, talking and laughing, looking colorful and alive and wonderfully modern against her Victorian surroundings. The solemn girl she'd dragged off with her was laughing, as well. Quinn had to look twice to be sure she was Patricia's step-whatever. Becky, who had all but disappeared in Patricia's shadow, was now walking confidently, eagerly answering a question Diana asked, and generally looking happy.

Had being around Diana done as much for him tonight? He suspected it had. Being around Diana lifted people's spirits. And he, for all his medical training and his business acumen, had no idea how she did it.

She fascinated him.

Quinn wished he'd had a chance to dance with her, but she'd clearly moved on to a new protégée for the evening.

"We're back," Diana said brightly.

Patricia cast a critical eye in her step-whatever's direction, then took a dramatically deep drink from her flute.

Quinn watched the young lady deflate a little, as if Patricia were the kryptonite to Diana's superpower. It was hardly young Becky's fault that Patricia's father's second wife had dumped her into Patricia's hands.

He smiled sympathetically at Diana's protégée. Becky would be all right. Diana had clearly taken her under her wing, and she'd have her dancing in no time.

The new Texas Rescue director was speaking. Her plans for the coming year were important, and her need for financial and facility support from the hospital were legitimate. Quinn could only lend her half an ear, however. The rest of him was distracted by details from his earlier conversations with Diana.

This would be much harder if you were a woman... you'd have to hope he asked you to dance.

It wasn't always good to have a mind that held details, endless details like Diana's description of the challenges faced by a woman who wanted to be asked to dance. When piecing together a medical puzzle, Quinn was grateful for his memory. Right now, it tugged at his conscience.

Patricia set her flute down and turned to him. "Now, would you dance with me?" she asked in her prettiest voice. She could be delightful company when she chose, but Quinn had known her too long and too well to be interested in more than friendship.

"Since your date is heading this way, I think he'll want this dance." It was a complete lie, of course, since Quinn hadn't caught sight of the missing Marcel, but damn it, Patricia had caused her ex-stepsister's spirits to droop, undoing Diana's good deed.

Quinn held out his hand toward the timid Becky. "Would you care to dance?"

The young lady brightened up once more and placed her hand in his. It wasn't the hand he wanted to be holding, and she wasn't the woman he wanted to dance with. But he'd made her happy by asking her to dance, which had in turn made Diana beam at him in approval. She even bounced on her toes, the tiniest of motions, reminding him of a kid at Christmas.

As Quinn led his partner onto the dance floor, he smiled. He'd made Diana happy, and damn if that didn't make him feel dangerously close to happy, too.

"Becky is a very nice person."

Diana waited for a reply, but Quinn's elegant friend barely made a polite noise of agreement.

Diana tried again. "Have you known each other long?"

Patricia Cargill, the woman who could be a match for Quinn, speared her with one direct look. "Long enough."

Not for Quinn.

Oh, Quinn could handle her, of that Diana had no doubt. In fact, Patricia needed a strong man like Quinn, someone she couldn't bully and intimidate. But Diana didn't want Quinn to have to spend his whole life shaping another woman's personality into something it naturally wasn't. Patricia reminded Diana too much of a striking but strong-headed Dalmatian they'd had a terrible time placing at the animal shelter. Eventually, a professional dog trainer had volunteered to work with families that expressed an interest in the dog, until they found one that could provide her the consistent discipline she needed without breaking her spirit.

I don't want Quinn to have to work that hard.

Quinn MacDowell was a nice guy. Diana hadn't even had to drop a hint, and Quinn had known right away that dancing with Becky would help make the ball beautiful for her.

Diana looked for her champagne glass, wanting a sip to privately toast Quinn, but the glasses were out of place.

"This one," Patricia said, and slid a flute toward her.

Diana took a sip. It was warm. And flat.

It was not real champagne.

She didn't like it. What a horrible realization, to know that forever more, she would not enjoy fake champagne. Quinn had introduced her to something better, and she couldn't undo that experience. Every interaction with every person left its mark, of course, so spending time with Quinn had been bound to affect her, but still...

Look on the bright side. You only got spoiled for champagne.

It could have been worse. She could have danced with Quinn.

It was a lucky thing that Patricia's arrival had saved her from having a taste of being Quinn's date for the night. Diana had never danced with a handsome man who wore a tuxedo as if it were a regular part of his wardrobe. A man who laughed as he poured champagne at a glorious gala.

She wouldn't miss what she'd never had.

Nothing had changed. Nothing at all. "Moonlight Serenade" had ended two songs earlier. Quinn was surrounded by friends, Becky was enjoying herself, and it was time for Diana to move on. Patricia would surely claim the next dance, and Karen looked like she was ready to talk business all night. Diana was feeling distinctly like the third wheel, now that Quinn was no longer a lone figure, brooding silently at a party.

Diana took another sip of the "domestic sparkling wine," as Quinn had called it, determined to be satisfied.

Patricia watched her. Her words were civil and smooth, but every muscle in her elegant body was tense. "You must have friends who are wondering where you are. Perhaps you should go back to them."

"I will," Diana said, fighting fire with friendliness, always her best chance at success. "I'll just say goodbye to Becky and Quinn and then I'll be on my way."

Patricia leveled a direct look on her, one that would have made many a puppy at the pound drop its gaze in submission. Diana kept smiling, anyway. Patricia looked away, toward the far side of the dance floor. "I see Quinn and Becky have joined a group of my friends. Karen, let me introduce you." She was already in motion before she casually spoke to Diana. "Do excuse us."

"Of course," Diana said, her smile firmly in place. *Easy girl, I'm not going to fight you for that bone. See how friendly I am? I'm just the buddy.*

But the buddy could hardly stand to watch, so Diana scooped up her tiny purse and retreated to the mezzanine once more, but not before topping off her sparkling wine with a tiny bit of the real champagne.

The buzzing of his cell phone gave Quinn the perfect excuse to leave Becky with a few of the young med school students who'd spent a month interning in his cardiology practice.

He stepped away from the group as he pulled the cell

phone from his pocket. The first digits of the phone number indicated that it came from one of the hospital lines.

"MacDowell," he said, turning his back on the orchestra.

"Quinn, it's Brian. Irene Caulsky passed away about twenty minutes ago. Thought you'd like to know."

"An MI?" Quinn knew it had to have been a heart attack, but he asked. It bought him a few seconds, the moments he needed to let that first punch of failure pass.

"Yes. She'd been sedated, but the nurses saw it happening on telemetry. I was on the floor when they called for the crash cart, so I stepped in. I think the nurses were relieved I was there to call it. Everyone could see this was the end."

"Of course. I'm glad she wasn't awake and aware." Modern medicine had its limits. The patient had already survived two heart attacks. Given her age and health, the odds of Irene surviving a third were practically nonexistent, but the hospital's floor staff didn't have the legal authority to declare a patient dead. They had to keep attempting to resuscitate a hopeless case until a physician could make the call. Since Quinn's new partner, Brian, had been present, everyone—including Irene's fragile, expired body—had been spared significant stress.

The orchestra finished its song, and the crowd applauded. Quinn hunched his shoulders to block out the sound as Brian told him the family had taken the news well. "They specifically asked me to thank you for taking care of their grandma."

Taking care of her. What had he done? He'd placed some stents in her arteries after the first heart attack. That had bought the octogenarian a few more years, until a second heart attack had brought her to West Central this morning, where Quinn had admitted her for an overnight stay in the critical care unit.

During those few years, she'd been a regular patient at the office as Quinn monitored the medicines he'd prescribed. She'd left his staff smiling after each appointment, because she called their boss "sonny boy" and she told all the women how beautiful and young they were. She'd never failed to ask Quinn how his mother fared.

He passed a hand over his eyes briefly. He'd have to call his mother tomorrow and break the news that her beloved fourth-grade teacher had passed away.

Brian's voice was clear as the orchestra struck up another song. "I'm sorry to bother you on your weekend off, but I thought you'd want to know about Irene."

"Thank you. I'm glad you were there, Brian."

"Me, too. I'll see you Monday."

Quinn disconnected the call, slid the cell phone back into his pocket and waited. The feeling of being punched would pass. It always did.

The human body cannot last indefinitely. This was a fact. It would always be a fact, no matter what cures were discovered and which diseases were eradicated.

Death is part of any medical practice. His earliest mentors had impressed that upon him. He'd chosen this profession knowing he would see death, up close and personal.

The patient died, but I did not fail to do my best. That was an important one. Quinn knew he'd done everything right. Everything was sometimes not enough. After all, the human body could not last indefinitely.

The loop of logical statements ran through his mind again, as they always did when he lost a patient, as they always did until his mind muted his emotions.

Quinn reached up to rub the back of his neck. This punch had been powerful, because Irene had been a special patient. The hurt wasn't subsiding at its usual pace. He focused on his surroundings, and realized he was staring at the potted palm trees Diana had hidden behind.

Diana. Quinn pictured her green dress and her shapely legs. For once, it was good to be able to recall the details: the way she'd bounced on toes that were polished in red and peeking through silver sandal straps. Impractical. Feminine. Sexy.

Diana—lively, lovely Diana. Quinn wanted to be with her. He wanted to hold her.

"Damn it, we were supposed to dance." He said the words under his breath as he turned back to the room, angry at himself for letting anything dissuade him from his earlier goal of dancing with Diana. With an intensity he could feel over and above the punch of losing a patient, Quinn wanted his hands on Diana. He wanted to feel that fringe in his fingers. He wanted to know the smell of her hair and the softness of her skin. He wanted that dance.

He looked toward the table where he'd left her standing with Patricia and the director of Texas Rescue. Only the champagne bottle remained.

She was gone. Again.

Chapter Four

Diana had barely reached the doors to the mezzanine when she ran into Dr. Lana MacDowell, the woman Quinn had been studying so longingly when Diana had first spotted him. Lana looked simply smashing in her evening gown, glowing like the bride she was as she walked next to Braden MacDowell.

Poor Quinn.

Diana held out her hand, ready to shake Lana's like a proper business associate, but Lana kissed her on the cheek and, to Diana's surprise, the always businesslike Braden did, too. They'd barely gotten past their hellos when a gentleman asked Lana to dance. Braden turned to Diana, and for the first time that night, she found herself on the dance floor, partnered by a handsome man in a tuxedo.

It was lovely. Diana enjoyed it for what it was.

Lovely—but not romantic. Even if Braden had been single, Diana would not have felt a spark with him. They were simply not a match.

She didn't recognize the song the band was playing. She wondered how Braden and Quinn were related—and she worried how Braden would feel if he knew Quinn was in love with his wife. She worried that Quinn would never get over his unrequited feelings for Lana. She worried—

"Are you having a good time tonight?" Braden asked.

"Yes, thank you."

Braden looked at her more closely. "Is anything wrong? That was the most lukewarm thing I've ever heard you say."

Diana felt herself blush a bit. This whole gala was to benefit the hospital that Braden's father had founded, the hospital he now ran as CEO. She'd gone and made him worry that she didn't like the evening.

She tried harder. "Nothing's wrong. Nothing *could* be wrong tonight. Your gala is absolutely beautiful, down to the last detail."

"Thank you, but I can't take credit for planning any of this. I only approved the final proposal." Braden smiled faintly at her praise, but he was still studying her too closely.

Diana seized on the subject of party planning and kept up a bright stream of chatter. She didn't doubt that she was rambling a bit, but people didn't mind in general, as long as she was friendly and undemanding.

The song ended, and they rejoined Lana just as Quinn walked up to their little group. Diana's bright chatter petered out. She couldn't talk around the lump in her throat as Quinn greeted Lana with a kiss on the cheek. When

Quinn and Braden stood side by side, Diana knew they had to be brothers.

Oh, God, poor Quinn—in love with his brother's wife. It made for dramatic movies, but in real life, she could hardly imagine a worse situation.

Braden introduced her to Quinn.

"Brothers?" Diana confirmed, then cleared her throat a little. "The green eyes threw me off. I should have seen the resemblance earlier."

"Earlier? You two have already met?" Lana squeezed Quinn's arm. "Diana's more than a real estate agent. She's a magician."

"She's already tried to perform a little magic with me tonight," Quinn said with mock severity. "Brace yourself. I've been dancing."

"No!" Lana laughed.

Quinn winked at Diana.

Two things hit Diana in rapid succession.

One, Quinn was not in love with Lana. It was evident in his body language, in his tone of voice, in his relaxed manner. Nope, not in love, not the least little bit.

Two, Diana was overwhelmingly relieved. Absurdly so. She wanted to laugh, to float, to hug everyone.

Quinn didn't need time to nurse a broken heart. He didn't need a transition girl.

He could—

What? Decide she was his perfect match? Choose her over all these elegant women as the one he wanted in his life?

Not very likely.

Her bubble burst. Diana tapped her purse impatiently against her bare thigh. It took courage to be happy, her mother had said. But experience had taught Diana that life was easier when you didn't expect too much. When you didn't long for things you couldn't have. When you enjoyed the sparkling wine, and didn't compare it to champagne.

What would one taste of Quinn be like?

She really should be going. It was time to move on. The MacDowells were catching up with each other. If she gave Lana a little friendly wave, if she nodded toward Quinn, then she could head to the mezzanine.

As she raised her hand for that wave, Quinn cupped her elbow. He stepped close to her, very close, and she was overwhelmed at the height and the heat of him, at his masculine body clad in a civilized tuxedo crowding into her personal space.

"You can't leave yet."

She looked up at him in surprise.

He smiled, a subtle lifting of one corner of his mouth. "I haven't had the privilege of dancing with you tonight."

Oh, this was delicious, this shiver his voice sent through her body. He sounded almost like he was giving her an order, but his words were so courteous. *The privilege of dancing with you...* She could get lost in a romantic fantasy if she weren't careful.

"That's okay. I've been forcing you to dance enough as is." She lightly socked him in the arm with her purse, as much to remind herself that she was his pal as for any other reason.

"I think my stamina is up to the task. Let's dance. This song fits you too well for us to stand here, talking."

Diana listened for a moment. Quinn thought "The Way You Look Tonight" fit her? This handsome man, the brother of people she liked and respected, liked the way she looked.

Life might never be this perfect again, her conscience reminded her. *You can't miss what you've never had.*

It takes courage to be happy. Diana remembered her mother's words. When in doubt, she always tried to follow her mother's advice. She placed her hand in Quinn's, and let him lead her onto the dance floor.

Quinn was a wonderful dancer, holding her properly with one strong arm across her back, just under her shoulder blades, making it easy for her to rest her entire arm along his. He held her other hand out to the side, keeping their arms extended like real ballroom dancers. Her hand rested easily in his. He held her with just the right amount of squeeze to make her feel secure.

Secure. Special. In sync. *Right.* Dancing with Quinn felt right. She looked up a bit, wanting to see his expression. Did he think they were a match?

"You were trying to escape again, weren't you?" he said, as they moved forward in time to the music.

With every step, her bare legs brushed the black wool covering his. Each and every step. She was aware of her relative nakedness in a way that made talking difficult. Or perhaps, it made talking imperative.

"You didn't need me any longer. Patricia was obviously your next dance partner."

"She is not the one I asked. You are."

Diana enjoyed that delicious shiver once more, before the implications set in. "So poor Becky is stuck with Patricia again? Oh—I don't mean your friend is someone to be stuck with."

"You meant exactly that, and you are exactly right." Quinn gave her a little extra spin at the edge of the dance floor, before they merged into the dance floor traffic once more. "Patricia can make a plant wither with one look, if she wishes. Never fear. I left Becky with some of West Central's med school students. They are much closer to her age, and they were fighting over the chance to dance with someone who isn't a professor's wife."

"That's wonderful. What a good idea."

She felt his fingers sift through the fringe that fell from her shoulder.

"Thank you," he said. "I'm not the magician you are, though. I'd like to know your secret. How did you change Becky's outlook so completely?"

Diana jumped at the chance to talk about something so silly. Remaining quiet as he toyed with the fringe of her dress was too much to ask of herself. Talking would distract her from this awareness of how they moved, how they meshed, how they made magic—at least in her mind. Oh, but did he feel it, too?

Talk. He asked about Becky.

She tapped his shoulder with her purse. "To my boss's dismay, this purse is too small for me to waste room on things like business cards, but I always find space for critical items like safety pins. Becky's dress was just a size too big. She couldn't relax, because her top was loose. A few safety pins along the seams—"

"Strategically placed while you chatted behind a palm tree?"

"Bingo. You can really dance once you know your dress won't come off."

Quinn laughed, but this time the laugh had a slightly different undertone. A little more bass to it.

"Since you're dancing with me, you must feel very certain that your dress is not going to come off."

She leaned back just enough to smile with him, but he wasn't smiling.

He turned them once more. "Your dress will stay on no matter what I try?"

The possibility that he was talking about more than dancing was hard to ignore.

Quinn spoke intimately into her ear. "I find myself tempted to test that theory."

He smiled at her, but it was something of a pirate's smile. "Just how certain are you that your dress won't be coming off tonight?"

Diana hoped her smile didn't slip. Apparently, she'd gone and done it again. A man had mistaken friendliness for something else. Something looser. Easier.

Sleazier.

She never saw herself that way. It always disappointed her when other people did. It just about killed her that Quinn did.

Darn it, she'd wanted him to be different.

She was curvy. She smiled a lot. Tonight, she was pretty much flashing all the leg she owned in a dress that was just a teensy bit too small. Could she blame Quinn for thinking she was less of a matchmaker and more of an easy bed partner?

She'd been thinking about finding magic, about making perfect matches. He was thinking about getting her naked. Tonight. His hand slid lower, leaving her upper back cold as he curved his arm around her waist.

The disappointment was crushing.

She started to let go. At the same moment she loosened her hold, he tightened his, and then she found herself bent backward in a dip, breathless and disoriented, despite being held securely by his strong arms.

The last notes of the song faded away. She focused on

his green eyes, the crystal and the flames and the music all a blur beyond him.

He smiled that disarming, charming half smile. "You were quite right. Your dress is secure. It's safe to dance the next song with me." He stood her up and gave her hand a friendly squeeze.

She was such an idiot. She was the one who'd jumped to all the wrong conclusions. They'd been talking about safety pins. Quinn hadn't been thinking of her in a sexual way; he'd been joking with her. Of course he had been—she was the buddy.

Quinn held her lightly, waiting for her to say she'd dance with him.

Diana called up her smile. She forced herself to laugh. She placed her hand on his shoulder and smacked her other hand in his, in a move that resembled a high five. "Let's dance. We can scope out your perfect partner over each other's shoulders."

Quinn knew he'd screwed up.

Thirty seconds, that was all it had taken. He'd been dancing with Diana, having a genuinely interesting and lighthearted conversation on a topic unfamiliar to him— how to fix a girl's dress and thereby a girl's evening— and then he'd lost Diana's spark. She was still dancing with him, moving in time to the music, but she was no longer *with* him.

He needed that spark. Without any conscious effort on her part, without knowing he was hurting from the passing of Irene Caulsky, she'd made him feel better. Balanced, like there was enough light in the world to offset the dark.

But somehow, he'd blown it. Hell, she was even looking for another woman again, someone else for him to dance with.

Quinn was familiar with situations that went sour in a moment. As a cardiologist, he'd had patients chatting groggily with him as they waited for their sedation to take effect suddenly go into full cardiac arrest. As a rancher, he'd seen livestock ambling across a dry creek bed, kicking up dust, suddenly be swept away in a roaring torrent of water, a deadly flash flood from some faraway rainstorm.

When situations turned, Quinn turned them back. He threaded wires into hearts and opened blocked arteries. He gave chase on horseback and lassoed swimming cattle.

What did he do with Diana?

Situations with women didn't turn so rapidly. Women liked being with him, and he with them. If a woman was upset, it was generally because he hadn't been able to keep a date—which usually meant a patient had taken one of those sudden turns for the worse. Although the circumstances that kept him from showing up were beyond his control, women liked an apology. They liked their apologies best when he showed up bearing a gift, generally wine and roses, or a tasteful piece of gold jewelry. No gemstones. He liked his relationships exclusive, but without expectations of permanence.

He wasn't in a relationship with Diana, and he hadn't failed to show up for this dance, but since women loved apologies…

"I'm sorry," he said.

Diana frowned slightly, making a little wrinkle appear between her brows. She really had a fascinating face, open and expressive. He wanted that genuine spark of hers to come back.

"I'm very sorry," he said, more emphatically.

"For what?" she asked.

That nearly made him pause in the middle of the dance floor. Women didn't ask that. They accepted his apology, took the wine and roses, and stayed with him.

Diana was different.

"For what?" he repeated, aware that he had no answer.

She met his gaze, and he noticed that although her eyes were brown, they had a touch of gold to them, or perhaps it was closer to copper, a bit of rose color to match her hair.

"All you did was dip me," Diana said. "Very nicely. You didn't even come close to dropping me."

They danced in silence while the band's singer crooned a few lines. Quinn thought back, trying to pinpoint where the tone of the evening had changed. "Perhaps I didn't give you enough warning? No one likes to be startled."

Her laugh sounded forced to him. "Seriously, Quinn, you've got nothing to apologize for. Look, there's that woman in the red dress again. No, don't look—that's too obvious. I'm looking for you. I don't think she's with any man in particular. You could dance us closer to her side of the floor, and then when the song ends—"

"I warned you, right before the dip, that I was going to test whether or not your dress was secure enough for dancing."

Diana abruptly fell silent. She studied the orchestra, keeping her face turned away from him.

Details. Quinn needed to remember the details. "I said... Aw, hell. I said I was going to try to get you out of your dress. That's it, isn't it? I didn't mean it that way, Diana. I'm sorry—truly sorry."

She looked at him for a second, but she seemed embarrassed, and she looked back at the band.

"I didn't mean it that way," he said, as lame an excuse as he'd ever given in his life.

"I know you didn't." She shrugged and spoke to his lapel. "I'm an idiot."

"Why are you the idiot? I'm the one who said something stupid." Quinn didn't like the way Diana seemed to assume she'd done something wrong. They'd stopped moving across the dance floor and were marking time, swaying to the music in one place. He tried to lighten the moment. "My mother would tan my hide if she heard me say such a thing."

"I took it the wrong way." She ventured a glance at him, embarrassment written all over her hide-nothing face.

Something in Quinn's gut twisted. "It was perfectly reasonable for you to have taken it that way. I imagine you've heard plenty of lines from plenty of men."

She blushed in the glow of the orchestra's stage lighting. "I know. My dress is too short, and I tend to touch people too much." She touched his shoulder with her purse, just one weak thump, a pale imitation of her earlier playfulness. "I give guys the wrong impression."

Quinn stopped cold, right there on the dance floor. "No. I meant nothing like that."

The song finished and couples all around them stepped apart. Their polite applause faded away as the band leader spoke. Diana dropped Quinn's hand and stepped back.

Damn it, he'd just told her she was wrong. He'd probably scared her with his intensity. This wasn't a hospital operating room. He didn't need to bark out corrections.

Diana was facing the band leader, looking interested in his words. Quinn stepped closer to her, so he could keep their conversation private. "The only impression you've given anyone tonight is that you are open and friendly."

Quinn had underestimated Diana, that much was certain. He'd thought she was an open book, unguarded almost to a fault, but she obviously had her past hurts and secrets. He tried, once more, to restore their lighter mood. "If I were making a pass at you, I would deserve a good, swift kick for a stupid line like 'bet I can get your dress off tonight.'"

"But you weren't making a pass at me, because we're just friends."

You weren't making a pass at me. She said it as though it were impossible for him to be interested. That she could miss his attraction to her was astounding.

Or perhaps, she did not want to see it, because she did not feel attracted to him. *We're just friends.* She'd made a point of saying that.

If a woman was not interested, then Quinn was not interested. After all, if the woman in white was not available, then the woman in blue or red would be. It had been so for as long as he could remember—since one cheerleader had broken his teenaged heart and two others had vied for the chance to make it whole. It made no sense for a man to hang all his hopes on one particular woman.

Unless that woman was one of a kind. Effervescent. Irresistible.

Diana tipped her chin toward a cluster of people grouped around a table. "I think you'll regret it for the rest of the weekend if you don't ask the woman in the red dress to dance at least once. The band leader just announced this was their last song."

She wanted him to find a new partner. Quinn felt that punch again. Loss. Diana Connor had no desire to get to know him better.

She was smiling at him, chatting away in that pleasant way of hers as she backed away. "I'm so glad I got to meet you tonight. I can honestly say I've never met a MacDowell I didn't like. Good luck with the lady in red. Now hurry, go."

He watched her as she began threading her way through the crowd around the edge of the dance floor. He remained stoic, waiting for cool logic to counter that hot stab of regret. The rationalizations began automatically: nothing lasted indefinitely. Endings were part of life. This loss hadn't occurred because he'd failed to do his best.

Quinn stopped the loop right there. Did he even know what his best was when it came to a woman? An apology. A piece of gold jewelry. A relationship with finite expectations. A civilized parting of ways after six months or twelve. That was the endless loop of his relationships, and it all required so little effort.

How could he let Diana walk away, when he didn't know what his best was?

Chapter Five

She wasn't going to cry. At least, not in public, she wasn't. Diana batted her eyelashes rapidly, heading for the mezzanine and the ladies' room, and nearly ran into the man in front of her.

He steadied her with a hand at her elbow.

Quinn. She knew it the instant before he spoke. "I meant it when I said you were the only woman I cared to dance with this evening, Diana. May I have the last dance?"

Quinn started guiding her onto the dance floor without waiting for her answer. Diana didn't try to resist. She'd never be the same after this ball, anyway. She'd never forget Quinn MacDowell, so she might as well enjoy the feeling of moving in time with him for a few minutes more.

She blinked her wet eyelashes some more, and gestured vaguely toward the spot where she'd left him. "How did you get in front of me?"

"You were going around the edges of the square, so I took the hypotenuse."

He was holding her with just the right amount of squeeze, moving the two of them easily to the music, and Diana felt like she could breathe without any danger of a sob coming out. Her smile was real. "Did you just use the word *hypotenuse* at a party?"

Quinn smiled, a full smile, the kind that lifted both sides of his mouth. *Dear Lord, he has a dimple on one side.*

"It's the shortest distance between two points," he said.

Diana rolled her eyes. "I can't believe your brain really works that way."

"Blame my father. I grew up on a ranch, and he taught me to ride at a forty-five degree angle to whatever path a runaway steer was taking."

She could be offended that he was comparing her to a steer, but it was too fascinating to imagine him as a boy on horseback.

"To cut off the steer's trajectory," he said, as if her silence meant he hadn't explained very well. "You can't chase behind them, you need to get in front of them, so they'll change direction and go back to the herd."

"You don't use a lasso?" Heck, if she was going to imagine Quinn as a cowboy, she might as well go all the way.

"That takes practice. I wasn't very good at it yet when my dad first took me on a round-up." Quinn shifted his arm, pulling her closer. "I doubt I'm good at it anymore, either. I spend all my time at the hospital."

"Your dad is a cowboy who taught you to think about a hypotenuse? He sounds very unique."

"He was. He's passed away."

"Oh, I'm so sorry." She squeezed his hand, the one he was holding in their ballroom dancing pose.

"Thank you. It's been years, I'm sad to say." He brought their joined hands closer to their chests, brushing his knuckles briefly over the curve of her cheek. "May I ask you why you were crying?"

Diana sucked in a quick breath at his caress, sorry he'd noticed her tears. She was supposed to make parties fun for everyone. "I wasn't crying."

"Technically, I suppose you weren't." He tucked their hands against his chest. The black satin of his lapel soothed the back of her hand as they danced, in silence. The music was beautiful, the lights were low, and her partner kept her secure as they danced smoothly, slowly, swaying to the sounds of an orchestra in a ballroom that had seen more than a hundred years of celebrations. It was one of the perfect moments of her life, and Diana knew it.

Gosh darn it, it was going to make her cry.

"Diana?"

She tilted her head back, looking at the blue sky that was permanently painted on the vaulted ceiling, as she blinked away more pesky salt water. "It's just a great evening, isn't it?"

"Yes, it is. That's making you sad?"

"I'm not sad. Beauty can make you cry."

They danced in silence a while longer, then Quinn spoke. This close, she could feel the deep bass of his voice in his chest.

"Were you experiencing great beauty as you left me so that I would dance with the woman in the red dress?"

"Oh, no fair. That's a hard question."

"It's a good question."

Diana tried to glare at him from under her wet lashes, but he seemed pretty unflappable. Darned doctor. He probably got training in that.

"Why don't you answer my good question? I'm very interested."

Honestly, how was a girl supposed to deal with a man like Quinn? *Honestly,* she supposed. The problem was, she wasn't really sure what was behind her tears. She did what she always did when faced with a dilemma, and started talking it out.

"My mother loved the performing arts. Ballet, symphony, plays." Diana could picture the list as her mother had written it, with loops for the tails of the letter *y* that were a work of art in themselves. "She said they were moments of perfection, and she was sorry I hadn't witnessed them with her, because they would never happen exactly the same way again. But she said I should go and find my own moments of beauty, and to have the courage to be happy, even knowing that happiness might only be a moment in time."

Quinn said nothing. The orchestra played, a beautiful blend of instruments. He held her against his polished tuxedo for the longest time, and then Diana felt him rest his cheek against her hair.

The song ended.

Diana closed her eyes, and tried not to care that a tear—or two, or three—fell from her lashes.

Mother knows best.

That last, sweet dance with Quinn had been special. Perfect. Her mother had been right: it was a moment in time that would never happen again, and it was all the more precious because of it. Diana wanted to quit while she was ahead.

She wanted to take her perfect memory of the perfect dance and go home, tuck both it and herself into bed, and relive it over and over. She'd even told Quinn she wasn't staying for the country-Western concert that was about to begin in the spacious mezzanine because she had to work this weekend. It was barely past ten o'clock, and Diana didn't have to be at the animal shelter at any particular time on Saturday, but she was expected, and it was work.

Before she left him, she had one more beautiful moment in mind, like something out of the movies. She envisioned herself leaving Quinn with a kiss, with one perfectly sweet press of her lips on his. Then she'd walk away, alone. But while she stared at his mouth, thinking about that kiss, his lips formed words she'd never expected.

"Where are you parked?"

She was undone by his practicality. She wasn't going to quit while she was ahead, after all. Quinn insisted on escorting her to her car, which seemed so very *Quinn* of him, Diana had not bothered trying to refuse. He'd already changed her image of the ideal man, setting the bar higher than she'd thought possible before tonight. She might as well take his arm and stroll outside on a summer night. It was a terrible risk, because no other summer night might ever be so special.

Quinn led the way through the crush in the mezzanine, nodding at acquaintances and subtly clearing the way as the crowd jockeyed for positions around the temporary stage. Diana spotted Becky Cargill, who was laughing as a young man boosted her onto a table for a better view as the evening's first star began his country-Western hit.

Diana smiled at Becky's happiness. There, at least, she'd lived up to her mother's standards. She was leaving someone at this ball better off than she'd found her.

Quinn kept Diana close behind him as they headed down to the lobby on the crowded, carpeted staircase. They were stopped by every other person, it seemed, people who wanted to greet Dr. MacDowell. Clearly, he was more important to the hospital than she knew. It was a sobering reminder that he was destined for a woman like Patricia Cargill, or the lady in red, or the woman in white. In the future, someone elegant and educated would accompany Quinn through event after elegant event.

Will she help him enjoy each party?

"Dr. MacDowell!"

Diana and Quinn turned simultaneously toward the woman who had called his name. There was something in the way she said his name, a tone of shock, that gave Diana chills.

"What are you doing here?" the woman asked, staring up at Quinn from the bottom of the staircase as if she couldn't believe her eyes.

Quinn hesitated, almost imperceptibly. Diana might have missed it if she hadn't had her hand on his shoulder, keeping her balance as she stood one step above him. Then, with his usual decisiveness, he led Diana down the last two stairs, pulled her out of the main stream of partygoers, and asked her to wait for him.

Diana watched him approach the woman. It was easy to see that he was saying "I'm sorry."

Everything about the woman's stiff posture expressed her shock. She kept looking from the phone in her hand to Quinn's face. "I just heard. You weren't there?" she said, her voice carrying easily above the motion and murmur of the lobby crowd. "But you're her doctor. You've always been her doctor. She loved you."

Quinn answered her, but he kept his voice too low for Diana to hear. Diana thought that was wise. She could tell in a glance that this woman was teetering on an emotional edge, and if Quinn raised his voice to match hers, she'd be high-pitched and howling in no time.

"You put her in the hospital and then you came to a *party?* You weren't there when she died?" The woman's words bounced off the marble and wood, drawing attention from those nearby, some of whom stopped and whispered to their fellows.

Diana's heart bled—for both the woman and Quinn. The woman was clearly distraught, but Quinn had to have been cut by that accusation, cut deeply. Still, he was staying calm, speaking seriously, giving the woman all his attention.

She jerked away from him. As she strode past Diana, she practically spat her words over her shoulder at Quinn. "I'm going to the hospital. You enjoy your evening, Dr. MacDowell. You just enjoy yourself."

Quinn said a few words to the man who'd been standing with her, who then headed after the woman.

Quinn remained where he was, looking calm and unfazed, when he couldn't possibly be. People began to resume their own conversations. Diana thought she should give him a minute, perhaps, to let him recover from the scene in his own way.

To heck with that.

Diana scooted around the people still lingering, perhaps waiting for more drama, and hugged Quinn's arm as soon as she reached his side. "I'm so sorry," she said.

He turned that neutral expression on her, then dropped his gaze to his sleeve, where she clung with both hands as she pressed against him. "For what? You have nothing to be sorry for."

"I'm sorry you had to hear such bitter words. She was in pain."

"Yes, she was. Her grandmother passed away this evening."

He sounded so matter-of-fact, but it was all so upsetting. Diana wished she could give Quinn a proper hug, but they were in a busy hotel lobby. At a black-tie gala.

Quinn covered one of Diana's hands with his. "It's an occupational hazard. I'm fine. Death is part of any doctor's practice. The human body can't last indefinitely. I did all I could."

"But—"

"Ready to leave?" Quinn turned toward the Sixth Street exit, as if he'd merely offered Diana his arm as a gentleman, not as if he had a woman clinging to him in sympathy.

She kept one hand tucked into his elbow. They were silent as they walked through the leaded glass door and down the steps to the sidewalk. The hotel anchored a corner of Sixth Street, a street lined with bar after restaurant after pub, each with its own musician spilling live music out its door. Diana was about to gesture one way, toward her car, when Quinn began walking her in the opposite direction.

It was Friday night, so the sidewalk was busy, filled with young people, hyper, happy, hollering, a striking contrast to the formal crowd in the hotel that loomed over them.

Quinn remained as he'd been all evening, calm, cool and collected in his tuxedo, walking with unhurried steps down Sixth Street, then down one of the main cross streets, but Diana was now certain his cool was all an act. Quinn MacDowell was upset: he'd forgotten to ask her which way to her car.

They lived different lives. They had nothing in common, not friends, careers or lifestyles. Diana would never have matched them together. It would have been as doomed as matching a Yorkie with a rancher. No matter how fond they were of each other, it was not a good pairing. As a couple, she and Quinn wouldn't last.

But tonight, he was more vulnerable than the world knew, and he had no one but her to care. He'd been alone when she found him, alone and brooding, and she wouldn't leave him just as badly off as she'd found him. Quinn MacDowell, M.D., needed her. And that, to her, was a thing of beauty.

Diana let him lead the way, content to go in the wrong direction with the right man.

Chapter Six

I did not fail to do my best.

No matter what her granddaughter had accused him of, Quinn had taken all the right steps with Irene. Quinn had assured her granddaughter that Irene hadn't suffered, although it would take time for that truth to sink in and bring comfort.

Quinn had done his best. It was a fact that the human body could not last indefinitely…

Diana rested her cheek on his shoulder, interrupting his thoughts and slowing his steps. Her simple act seemed tender. Sweet—to cancel out the bitterness.

If Quinn allowed himself to think about that, he'd lose what calm he commanded.

Yet, he was glad she was by his side. As her hair brushed his cheek, he could abandon logic and loss, and lose himself in the sensation of having a woman so willingly pressed against him. She smelled good, damned good, a mix of flowers and spices, a feast for the senses. Quinn allowed himself to breathe more deeply, long, slow inhalations that matched their unhurried steps. More spicy than floral, he decided, like the best wine in his collection.

Quinn glanced down, taking in the view of her legs from this angle. They stepped in unison over each crack in the sidewalk, the metallic straps of her sandals reflecting the neon lights of the bars they passed. The rhythmic flashes of her bare legs and the flexing of her toned thighs had a hypnotic effect that silenced the endless loop of his thoughts.

They were alive, she and he. The human body had its limits, but it also had its pleasures, and hers was a pleasure to view. From the first moment she'd sat next to him and he'd watched that green hemline settle dangerously high on her thighs, Quinn had been enjoying the view.

For hours, he'd watched as she'd smiled and laughed, beautifully enjoying her life. And Quinn? Hell, he'd had to be told that a ball was made for dancing, that sparkling wine was worth drinking, that a man should find the right woman.

The right woman. What did that mean? A woman whose willingness to be happy made those around her happier. A woman with childish delight in a party. A woman with a wise appreciation of the ephemeral quality of beauty. A woman who outshone the shimmer of her own silk-fringed dress.

Watching her was no longer enough. Not nearly enough.

The night was still young, and Quinn was wasting this time with her, settling for a glimpse of leg, a whiff of fragrance, a hand on his arm. It was all too little, a drop of water on the tongue of a man who'd just realized he was dying of thirst.

He dropped his arm, sliding it around her waist to pull her closer. Better. They kept walking as she slid her arm around his waist, too, and he turned to kiss her temple, savoring the warmth as he pressed his mouth to her skin. She pressed her whole body against him in response, and the last of Quinn's reason took a hike.

They'd reached his building. Thank God. It would only be minutes before he could satisfy his craving for Diana. The elevator was mirrored, and it would soon be filled with reflections of tan legs and red-gold hair. He'd get his hands on all that green fringe, get his mouth on hers. They'd lose his jacket, shred the tie, and by the time the elevator stopped on his floor, he could have her in his condo and on his bed in—

He stopped at the lobby doors, pulled her into his arms, and kissed her on the sidewalk, because the elevator was too far away. Her mouth was perfect, hot and moist and as eager as his. He pulled her body against his, and her arm felt strong around his waist. They were alive. They were together.

Her other hand slid over his collar and secured a fistful of his hair.

Hell, yes.

The crowd on the sidewalk approved, too. The wolf whistles barely registered, but when male voices got too close and too crude, a sense of protectiveness made Quinn break off the kiss. Diana's expression was perfect. Panting, a bit dazed, she looked at him with something close to wonder—exactly how he felt.

Awed.

"You are…my God, Diana, you are everything worth having. Kissing you, it's…"

"It's magic," she whispered. "I know."

He pushed open the glass door to his building and waited for the security guard to recognize his face and buzz him through the inner set of doors.

"Why are we going in here?" Diana asked.

"I live here."

"Good."

She grabbed him by the lapels and kissed him hard. She was a great kisser, matching him in intensity, meeting him all the way. When the buzzer sounded, Quinn backed into the inner door, dragging Diana into the lobby with him before he dragged his mouth away from hers.

That elevator seemed a mile away. As they crossed the carpeted lobby, he grabbed one end of his bowtie and jerked it loose. The elevator doors opened with a soft chime. He took one step inside, managing—just barely—not to yank her into the mirrored interior. He forced himself to turn and place a hand on the door to prevent it from sliding shut.

Diana hadn't stepped in when the door opened. She was looking over her shoulder, taking in the artwork, which was set off by the dramatic architecture of the lobby. With his eyes on her legs, he saw her bounce, just once, on her toes. "This is a beautiful place."

Control. He needed control over himself. He took her hand, brought it to his lips, and kissed the flawless, smooth skin. "I can't see it. I only see you." It was sappy. He'd never been more serious.

She looked at him, her brown eyes serious, too. "Let's make some magic," she whispered.

He didn't move.

"Now."

He yanked her into the mirrored car and slammed the side of his fist on the *close door* button. She didn't need to regain her balance, because he lifted her high against him as the doors slid shut. He devoured her mouth as he cupped her perfectly rounded backside in his greedy hands. Her purse hit the floor and her hands dug into his shoulders as she wrapped one leg around him, and he felt the heel of her silver sandal pressing into the back of his thigh.

He tore his mouth away from hers, struggling to slow the pace—he was not going to take her in the elevator, no matter what his body demanded—but when he opened his eyes, he saw Diana everywhere, every angle, wrapped around him like a dream come to life. The green dress had finally, finally ridden above the perfect curve of her backside, and his hands were spread over hot-pink satin. Color, vibrant color. That was Diana, beautiful, vibrant Diana.

The chime sounded again, and she quickly let go of him to slide down his body until her toes touched the ground again. People were waiting outside. Quinn instinctively stepped in front of Diana, although he was aware that the mirrors probably hid nothing.

"Quinn," one of his neighbors greeted him, getting on without waiting for Quinn to get off.

He could feel Diana wriggling behind him to pull her dress down as two more guys stepped inside.

"You going to the roof party?" one asked.

"No," Quinn said, and he hit the *door open* button while the look on his neighbor's face registered a big moment of enlightenment as Diana slid into a deep knee bend to pick up her purse, using Quinn's leg for balance.

"Right," the man said. "Catch you later."

They left, Quinn keeping Diana close behind him in the hallway as the elevator continued without them.

"Are you okay?" he asked. The words "I'm sorry" were on his lips when he realized Diana was laughing.

And so, suddenly, was he. Life was good. This night was perfect. This woman was amazing.

He scooped Diana into his arms and carried her down the hall to his door. She pulled her jeweled barrette out of her hair, and shook out surprisingly long hair. Quinn managed to open his door as he cradled her to his chest, because she was unbuttoning the studs of his tuxedo shirt, and there was no way in heaven or hell he'd stop her from doing that.

Quinn carried her over his threshold and, without pausing, straight into his bedroom. They didn't need to discuss anything. Shoes were kicked off, protection was grabbed from a drawer and Diana pushed him down on his own bed to finish undressing him. He lay on his back, drowning in a sensual feast of spice and flowers, held captive under the fall of her hair. She didn't make him wait before she straddled him, and he, with a lift of his hips, was desperately, insanely grateful to bury himself in the welcoming warmth of this woman.

And later, much later, as he drifted off to sleep with Diana in his arms, Quinn knew Diana had worked her magic.

For this moment in time, he was truly, unreservedly happy.

"You're running away again, aren't you?"

Diana froze in the middle of pulling on her sandal, achieving a moment of perfect balance on one foot, something that would have made any yoga instructor proud. Then she finished tugging her ankle strap into place with a precarious hop. Darn it, she'd been so quiet, gathering up her clothes and tiptoeing into the living room to get dressed, buying time while she tried to figure out what the proper morning-after etiquette ought to be.

Her time to decide was up. She straightened and faced Quinn. He was standing in the archway that separated the hall from the living room, leaning with one arm high against the wall, as if he'd been there, watching her get dressed, for some time. He was very nearly naked. Stunningly, wonderfully nude, except for skintight black boxer-briefs that did almost nothing to hide his athletic body. His half-aroused, athletic body.

She couldn't help but gaze for a moment at thick calves, hard abs and sculpted biceps, amazed that she'd had a man like that at her mercy, even for one night. When she finally looked at his face, his knowing expression made her blush.

She turned her back to him, although her dress was unzipped in the back, so her move revealed more of her body, not less. In the cold light of day, it was hard to feel like a woman who could make demands of a man. She was just Diana Connor, small-potatoes real estate agent, matchmaker at the dog pound, everybody's favorite pal.

Last night had been a breathtaking experience, one of those beautiful moments in time, and she was glad she'd had the courage to enjoy it while she could. She started to fumble with her zipper, trying not to cringe at her own thoughts. Her mother had undoubtedly never intended her *it takes courage to be happy* philosophy to apply to sex with a stranger.

He is a MacDowell, though, Lana's brother-in-law. He isn't really some stranger from a bar.

She yanked at her zipper, feeling defensive against her own accusations.

"Let me help you with that." Quinn walked up behind her and stilled her awkward hands with his own. He began zipping her dress, but stopped in the middle of her back to scoop her long hair out of his way with sure hands, the hands of a doctor, hands that had twisted a napkin around a champagne bottle before teaching her how good something could taste.

He took his time smoothing her uncombed hair over her shoulder. Diana held very still, melting under that soothing touch. The touch of a cowboy? She felt like a skittish horse.

"Where were you going?" he asked.

"Remember, I told you at the Driskill that I had to leave because I had work today?"

He took her by the shoulders, gently, and dropped a kiss on the nape of her neck. "You were going to leave without saying goodbye."

She shivered, and she knew he felt it. "Isn't that how it's done? No expectations, no strings attached, no embarrassing morning-after moments?"

For the teeniest, tiniest piece of a second, she thought she felt his fingers tighten on her shoulders, but he sounded perfectly calm and certain when he spoke. "Not after a night like ours. You told me there were moments of beauty that could make you cry. Believe me, Diana, you had me as close to tears as I've ever been." He turned her to face him. "You don't sneak out after a night like that."

He was so ridiculously handsome, so confident in everything he said. How could he expect so much from her?

"I didn't know that rule. I don't do one-night stands." She gestured to her dress apologetically. "I know you might find that hard to believe."

He narrowed his gaze, causing lines to form at the corners of his eyes. They weren't laugh lines. "What do you mean, I'd find that hard to believe?"

Diana couldn't bear the scrutiny of that green gaze. She stepped away. "I don't usually show this much skin. I was trying to look glamorous, like I belonged at the gala, maybe like I was rich." She gestured at the modern space of his living room, with its sky-high ceilings and industrial beams.

She'd seen condos in this building hit the real estate listings. They started just under a million. She'd never shown one to any of her clients. This wasn't her world. She hadn't even known what she was pretending to be.

"But I didn't look glamorous, did I? Not like your friends in their gowns. I just made myself look like a girl who…will. And I did."

Diana studied Quinn's million-dollar modern industrial designer fireplace until she couldn't take the silence and looked at him. He'd crossed his arms over his chest, but was otherwise scrutinizing her the same way as before, green eyes, serious expression. She let her own gaze drop to his chest, with its defined muscles, and to his flexed arms. Already, it seemed incredible to her that she'd ever made love to a man that looked like that. That she'd made a man like him gasp and shudder at her touch. She couldn't have missed what she'd never had, but now that she'd been with Quinn, how would she fantasize about anyone else, ever again?

Quinn abruptly uncrossed his arms and closed the space between them. "Okay, let's get two things sorted out. First, you do not look like the kind of girl that guys think *will*. You look like the kind of girl that guys *wish* would, but they know won't. There is an innocence about you that's as obvious as your beauty."

He turned her around, she assumed in order to finish tugging up her zipper. Instead, she felt him run one finger over her bra strap. "Do you know what I was thinking right now, watching you put on this pink underwear? It looks like one of those old-fashioned bathing suits from the World War Two era. That fits you perfectly. You're the kind of girl men painted on their bombers, the kind of girl that would give a man a reason to fight to get home. Sexy, but smiling. You're a bombshell, Diana, but with that girl-next-door friendliness. I am very, very lucky to be with you. Do we have that straight?"

She nodded, speechless around the lump in her throat. She loved the image of herself he'd just painted. Loved it.

"Good, then are you ready to address the second thing?" He zipped up her dress in one efficient move.

She faced him, waiting. He didn't look so stern now.

"You don't do one-night stands. I don't, either." He imitated her earlier gesture, the one she'd made to indicate her short dress, brushing his hand over his own bare thighs. "I really don't, although I know you may find that hard to believe, considering how I'm dressed."

He smiled at her then, and surprised a laugh out of Diana. Really, he was so charming when he wasn't brooding.

"This isn't a one-night stand yet," he said. "It will be if you leave and never see me again. For the sake of not ruining our track records, we should stay together for a while longer, don't you agree?"

He pulled her into his arms, and she hugged him, fitting against his body easily. He kissed her, a leisurely taste as different from their aggressive passion as day from night. Different, but wonderful all the same. Last night, he'd been in a civilized tuxedo, but he'd been more demanding. Today, he was all bared body, but a gentleman.

His mouth left hers to trail along her jawline, to nuzzle aside her hair, until he whispered in her ear. "If we make love today, then last night wasn't a one-time thing. And if we promise to make love tomorrow, then we can say we've been dating, and no one will think we're shallow."

"Or sleazy," she said, whispering in his ear.

"No, we don't want to be sleazy. Anything but that."

He lowered her zipper, gave her dress a tug so that it fell to the floor. She stood there, feeling glamorous and glorious in her bombshell bathing suit underwear.

With an almost unbearably light touch, Quinn traced one finger over the contours of her pink bra, from her shoulder to the tip of her breast. As he slid his palm slowly over the satin covering her backside, she whispered her next words over his lips.

"We better get started. I want to be sure I'm a respectable woman by the time I get to work at the shelter."

Chapter Seven

The animal shelter was Quinn's idea of hell. Sheer, unadulterated, headache-inducing, noisy hell. And it smelled bad, too.

Diana seemed oblivious to her horrible surroundings. She'd just left the building with a family of four whose youngest son was cradling a dog that weighed as much as he did. It was quite possibly the ugliest dog that Quinn had ever seen, but the boy was pampering it like it might win a blue ribbon at the Westminster, and Diana was beaming like—well, like the successful matchmaker she was.

She didn't even get paid for this. She just liked it.

How could anyone like this? The cinder block reception building had a red door that led to the parking lot and a blue door that led to a long walkway lined with kennels for the larger dogs. Quinn loathed that blue door.

The moment it opened, every dog erupted into a barking frenzy. He'd given up trying to speak after the first two rounds. It took at least eight long minutes for the dogs to calm down, every time. He'd timed it.

There was one dog that never calmed down. For two hours, he'd listened to either that one dog barking, or fifteen. Quinn had missed hearing his own phone ring, something that was more than an irritation. He was a cardiologist. He was on staff at a hospital. He served with Texas Rescue. His calls were no joke.

Granted, Brian was on call this weekend to handle his private practice patients, but that didn't mean Quinn could go off the grid and be completely unreachable. Whether he wore a tuxedo or scrubs or today's jeans and cowboy boots, he was a doctor, and he had responsibilities. Always. He'd tried to return a missed call from Brian three times, but each time he hit the call button, someone would touch that damned blue door, and the frenzy would begin.

He'd tried standing outside to place calls in the nearly one-hundred-degree heat, but the dog kennels were open-aired. Shaded, but open to the air, and noisy as hell. At least the lobby was air-conditioned and noisy as hell.

He leaned back in the plastic patio chair that served as lobby furniture, tempted to bang his head on the cinder block wall behind him, until he realized silence reigned. The dogs had finally calmed down, now that Diana had taken the family and their large creature out to the baking-hot parking lot. The solo barker had even gone silent. Quinn quickly got out his cell phone.

No sooner had he tapped Brian's name to initiate the call than a volunteer, a teenager who didn't appear to be

the sharpest knife in the drawer, meandered to the blue
door and reached for the knob.

"Don't touch that damned door."

The teen barely flinched, but he did glare at Quinn
as he shoved his hand into the front pocket of his shred-
ded jeans. "Dude, you need to chill."

Quinn came out of his chair, and the teen showed
some normal sense of self-preservation, backing away
from six feet of grown man in his prime. Angry grown
man.

"Dr. MacDowell here," he barked into the phone when
his practice's answering service picked up. He considered standing in front of the door in case the surly teen
wanted to make a second, defiant attempt at the knob,
but the kid retreated to the side room that held a wall of
stacked kennels for little dogs.

*Good. Let him sit in there and listen to the Chihua-
huas yip.*

Just as the answering service relayed Brian's mes-
sage to him, Diana came in from the parking lot. The
opening of the red door meant the blue door rattled at
the incoming rush of hot summer air, and the dogs went
berserk again.

"Another happy family," Diana announced.

Quinn cursed under his breath and tossed his phone
on the counter.

Diana looked only slightly less wary of him than the
teenager had. "Where's Stewy?" she asked.

"He's in with the little dogs."

"Shoot. I asked him to start leashing the dogs that
were due for their walk."

Quinn had undoubtedly stopped him from doing
just that.

The dogs were only one minute into their eight-minute frenzy. He scrubbed his jaw with one hand. Ol' Stewy had been right. He needed to chill, because he was stuck. He'd offered to drive Diana here, so he couldn't leave until her shift was over.

He shouldn't have driven her here. After this morning's lovemaking, another round of sex so perfect it was humbling, he'd been right to drive her to her car, of course. Then he'd followed her to her house, one of the funky 1940s bungalows that made up various Austin streets. Diana's street had been a mix of decrepit buildings and absurdly cute restorations. Her unique house had been in transition from one to the other.

While she dressed for the day, he'd waited in a living room the size of a postage stamp. He'd begun handling the day's requirements by calling his mother to break the news of Irene Caulsky's passing. His mother had assumed he was calling to find out if she needed anything for the afternoon's family get-together.

He'd forgotten all about it. It wasn't like him to forget a commitment, but his body was conveniently ruling his brain, he supposed. He started mentally adjusting his plans. It took an hour to drive to the ranch, plus he'd need to stay for two hours. Add in the hour return, and he'd lose four hours out of the weekend he'd planned to spend not having a one-night stand with Diana Connor.

Taking her to the ranch with him was out of the question. Introduce a girlfriend to his mother? He might as well buy a diamond ring if he was going to raise everyone's expectations that way. He had to be particularly careful with Diana. She wasn't from his usual crowd. She might not understand that a professional with a career like his had no time—and no desire—to be anything other than a bachelor.

No, if he couldn't spend the whole day in bed with her, then a straightforward dinner date and a return to his place would be the right thing to do. Keep it clear. Keep it simple.

Then Diana had emerged from her bedroom. She'd been telling the truth when she'd said that she didn't usually show as much skin as she had at the gala, but that didn't mean she wasn't as sexy as hell in her casual Saturday clothes.

Her red denim shorts were nearly knee-length, but they were skintight. Her short-sleeved button-down shirt, white with cherries printed all over it, was tucked firmly into her waistband and buttoned up high enough so it didn't show a hint of what he knew from firsthand experience was first-class cleavage. Despite the casual white canvas sneakers on her feet, her shirt sparkled with red sequins, one in the middle of each cherry. The red rhinestone sunglasses perched on her head were overkill, but even so, Diana looked like one of those 1940s pinup-girl posters. A poster that some kid had glued sequins all over, but still a picture to fuel a man's fantasies.

Quinn had taken one look and known he wasn't willing to say goodbye for four hours. Not yet.

They'd eaten a quick lunch at a food truck on the way to her beloved animal shelter. He'd planned on stealing touches and kisses and enjoying more of the way Diana had teased him at the gala. Instead, he'd gotten a headache from the dogs and the chaos, and he'd resented each and every person who'd taken Diana's time and attention away from him.

The dogs launched into their second minute of noise. Six more to go.

He hadn't expected to be unable to work. He hadn't expected that Diana would do nothing *but* work.

"I stopped Stewy as he was going to leash them up," he said, using a voice that would carry over the barking. "My fault. I needed him to hold off so that I could get one phone call in. One."

Just one godforsaken phone call in this madhouse.

Diana walked straight to him and gave him a hug.

Damn. It was a little alarming, the way she did that, but he had to admit it was an effective way to break the tension that had been stretching between them for the past two hours.

Quinn hugged her back, and the feel of her body against his lightened his mood considerably. Hadn't she taught him to look on the bright side? He'd make love to this woman tonight—and tomorrow, too. They had a commitment to that much, and despite this canine chaos being her idea of fun, he wanted to uphold his end of that bargain. Badly.

She let go of him and picked up the first leash. With that uncanny prescience she had, she correctly interpreted his pain from the cacophony of dogs. "You hate the noise, I can tell, but don't worry. They'll be quieter after their walk."

As she gathered up the rest of the leashes, he enjoyed looking at her fully clothed, knowing what she looked like naked. It was an incredible turn-on to know that those white sneakers hid pretty toes, painted red. Anyone could see that she had a nicely curved backside in her red denim, but he'd actually felt the smooth skin, felt the muscle flex beneath his hand.

The red door opened again, the blue door rattled and the dogs went crazy, a welcome distraction for once, since Quinn's thoughts had been about to cause a physical reaction that would be distinctly uncomfortable right now.

Another man entered the shelter. With her back to him, Diana didn't see the older man checking her out, but Quinn caught it. He retrieved his phone, slid it into his pocket, and then stood with his arms crossed over his chest, staring the man down. It took less than two seconds to make his point silently. Quinn had inherited his dad's build, as had his brothers. It was useful.

The door opened again—the dogs kept up their cacophony—and more people entered, Austin hipsters by the look of them. Diana had warned him that Saturday was their busiest day. The men in this new group also did a double take at Diana. Quinn kept his stance, acting like her bodyguard.

He wasn't really irritated with other men looking. It was impossible not to look at someone as pretty as Diana. But judging from her insecurity this morning, men had obviously made comments in the past, comments that embarrassed her, and that would not happen while Quinn was around.

She seemed oblivious to her appeal. Quinn watched her give instructions to the man who'd arrived alone, who was yet another volunteer. Diana was surprisingly organized, or perhaps it was only that she was experienced. Either way, she displayed a competence he hadn't expected with her party-loving persona. In fact, for the past two hours, she'd seemed like the only competent worker here. Her patience with the other volunteers amazed him, although he found that less surprising.

After all, she'd been amazingly patient with him as he'd glowered at the gala.

"Now that Bill is here, would you like to walk the dogs with me?" she asked Quinn. "We could get them all done at once. The sooner they're walked, the sooner I'll be done for the day."

Quinn began leashing up barking dogs.

They only walked about fifty yards to a fenced area where the dogs were to run free. Some valiant, heat-defying cedar elm trees provided shade. At the park, Quinn hated to unleash the dogs after the amount of time they'd spent getting them on the leashes, but he did.

Diana took the leashes from his hand and hung them on the gate. Her whiskey-colored hair looked more red today, perhaps because of the cherries and the red sunglasses. Perhaps it was an effect of the June sunlight. Quinn had a sudden desire to make love to her while the sun was high in the sky, just to experience her at her most vibrant color.

"I didn't realize you weren't a dog person," she said. The way she studied the leashes, refusing to make eye contact, belied her casual tone. She was frowning. Quinn realized that while he'd kept his mind firmly on their physical compatibility, she'd been thinking about something else completely.

He should have realized what was at stake here. Dogs were important to her. Hating what a woman loved was not the way to convince someone to get naked under a hot summer sun.

"I don't hate dogs," he said automatically. He wished the words back immediately. They were so obviously a knee-jerk response, and they were in contrast to the way he'd been acting for the past two hours.

She made a sound, a *tch* of disappointment, or disapproval, or even anger, that made Quinn feel cold. Had he just lied to her? He wasn't the kind of desperate guy that would say anything to get a woman into bed. He wasn't.

He watched the pack of ecstatic mutts. They looked like they were in a normal environment, running free like this. More like the dogs he'd grown up with. He needed to dig a little deeper, if he wanted Diana to believe him.

"I've always had dogs, but they're free to roam the ranch."

"Like a pack of wild animals?"

"No. Like ranch dogs." Quinn didn't want her to think so poorly of him. He reached for some details, the kind of details a dog lover would care about. "You almost can't have a ranch without some good dogs. One or two always choose to live in the barn. They keep the horses calm. Sometimes, a particular horse and dog will get on so well, they become a constant pair. The dog comes along every time you take the horse out."

"Like animal best friends? That's adorable."

Quinn didn't think any cowboy had thought of a barn-dwelling dog in those terms. Still, Diana wasn't frowning any longer. He kept talking.

"We had one dog we called the porch dog. He decided that was where he belonged. Mom liked him, because he kept the armadillos out of her flower beds. Most of the dogs are self-appointed patrolmen, though. They almost never barked, so when they did, you took notice. It meant a stranger was coming—or once, we went to see what they were barking at, and found a horse had broken his leg in the pasture and was struggling like mad. My dad had to put him down." Jeez, he hadn't thought about that in years. It had been a hard day in his boyhood.

She squeezed his arm, a little hug. "You do like dogs. It's the barking that gets to you. The kennels must have been hard today."

"Of course that noise was irritating. I couldn't make any calls. I got zero work done."

"My guess is that somewhere inside you is a boy who was raised to know that barking meant danger. It must have driven you crazy to hear dogs bark for two hours. I'm so sorry to have put you through that."

He'd never dated a woman so soft, so sympathetic. It was sweet, but once more, she was apologizing for something that wasn't her fault. It bothered him now as it had last night. "I would have left and come back later if it really was that bad. The truth is, no matter how annoying that barking was, I wanted to stay with you."

"Really?"

She seemed very happy with him now, and Quinn felt good, too. Damned good. Being around Diana could get addicting.

"I'm flattered that you and the little boy you once were wanted to be with me that much." She kissed him then, sweetly, but with her pinup-girl body pressed against the arm she was hugging.

Quinn broke off the kiss first. "I have to warn you, there's nothing boyish about what I want to do with you, but if flattery gets me anywhere, by all means, be flattered." He took the red glasses off her face and angled in for a better, closer kiss. Harder. One with more passion, one that led him to press her back to the fence.

Her passionate response blinded him, all heat, all sunshine, until a dog jumped on her, dirty paws on her white

cherry blouse. Quinn had him off in a second with a snap
of his fingers and a sharp verbal command.

"Wow, you did that like a pro," Diana said, taking her
sunglasses back from his hand.

Quinn snapped a leash on the dog, then whistled to
see which others would respond. It was all coming back
to him. He hid a smile as two more dogs ran up, tails
wagging as he leashed them. "I told you, I don't hate
dogs. I've got lots on my ranch."

Diana made little kissing noises to get a few more
dogs to come her way for their leashes. "It sounds wonderful. A real ranch, then."

"As opposed to what kind?"

"Some people say they live on a ranch, but what they
mean is they live in a ranch-style house on a two-acre
lot."

"This is a real ranch. The dogs there all have a purpose. I think that makes them content."

"You're so, so right. Even city dogs need a purpose.
These guys might not have ranching skills, but they'd
love the job of being a companion. They just need the
right person to make them happy."

All the dogs had been leashed but one. Quinn could
tell that mischief-maker wasn't going to come, no matter how much he whistled or Diana smooched. Quinn
knew what was coming next. "I suppose I'm supposed
to chase him down like I'm in a greased pig contest?"

Diana laughed at that. "We can just wait. He'll wear
himself out sooner or later, the way he's running around."

"How long does that usually take?"

"Half an hour or so."

Quinn suspected she winked at him when she said
that, but she'd put her sunglasses on. Visions of mak-

ing love in the sun flashed through his rather one-track mind. He had to get to the ranch soon, but if the dog didn't waste half an hour, maybe he could put that time to good use first.

"I'll catch him," he said, properly motivated by the possibilities.

What ensued, however, was the rather humbling adventure of trying to corner a smart dog who thought this was all a grand game. It would have been hellish, except for the fact that Quinn had the sexiest cheerleader in cherries rooting for him.

"Hypotenuse, Quinn!" she shouted. "Take the hypotenuse!"

He laughed as he slipped and slid, changing directions until he actually cornered the beast—who proceeded to slobber affection all over him.

Diana could dish out the sarcasm as well as his brothers could. She'd love his brothers. Or rather, she'd love Jamie, the one she hadn't met yet. Braden already thought she was something special. Diana would go crazy for the ranch dogs. She'd love his mom's sweet tea. She'd love his ranch.

As his innocent pinup girl laughed at him under a clear blue sky, nothing seemed more reasonable than sticking to his original plan of spending the whole day with her. Diana would love the ranch. Why not take her there?

It would be no big deal to bring his first girl home to the River Mack Ranch—and to Mom.

Chapter Eight

"This is such a big deal," Quinn's mother whispered fiercely. "If I'd known you were bringing a girl home, I would have made a cake, at least."

"This isn't a big deal, Mom." But Quinn had been delusional to think otherwise. "I just wanted Diana to meet the dogs. Maybe the horses. I don't know if she likes horses."

"Go ask her. Show her the barn. You have plenty of time before we eat."

Despite the fact that he'd given his mother no warning about bringing a guest, she was delighted with him. He didn't have the heart to tell her, once more, that this was just a date, not a commitment of any kind, in any form.

Diana, at least, was taking it all in stride. She'd been happy to see Lana and Braden, pleased to meet Kendry and Jamie. Quinn walked her through the stables and out the far side, and then he kept walking with her, because they were talking and there didn't seem to be any reason to stop. Diana had liked the horses, but she'd made a bigger fuss over Jamie's baby, Sam. It was Quinn's mother, however, that seemed to have made the biggest impression on her.

"She's so very pretty at her age, don't you think? Of course you must think so. But your mom really is. I love her apron, and the sweet tea. You're so lucky, having a good cook for a mom. Do you come out here every weekend? I would, just for the food."

They walked on, staying along the fence line and the hundred-year-old live oaks. It was hot, but not stifling, and Quinn found himself seeing the ranch through her eyes, really looking at it for the first time in years. In a decade. The house was behind them, easy to spot where it stood on its slight elevation, a beacon of white symmetry with a wraparound porch. The stable was aged wood, almost as large as the house. The pastures were green, but they'd turn brown when they baked all summer long in the ovenlike heat of Central Texas.

This was his heritage, this ground they strolled over. The ranch dogs served as a distant escort, running away to check on some smell, returning to see how far the humans had progressed. It had always been so, Quinn realized. He'd never walked the ranch alone, but always had dogs nearby. He'd taken that canine company for granted.

He could have a dog in his condo. There was plenty of room for one of Diana's strays, and he had no doubt she'd match him up with a dog of the right temperament. As soon as he thought it, cool logic countered the thought. He had room, yes, but he had a doctor's unpredictable schedule. As the owner of a private practice, he worked far more than a forty-hour workweek. Between office hours and hospital rounds, between board meetings and cardiac caths, he worked closer to seventy hours, on average.

He could not have a dog, even if he wanted one. He wouldn't be so inconsiderate, to have another life depending on him for companionship he couldn't give on a daily basis.

As they walked under the oaks, Quinn watched for roots that could trip them. Diana looked around, silent after singing his mother's praises, with a bit of her ever-present smile on her lips. Her lips were made for kissing. He'd like to have her around for kissing on a daily basis.

Cool logic intruded once more. He didn't have time for a girlfriend, either. It would be difficult to find time for Diana next weekend. He could visualize his calendar, remember the details. Two weeks from now, his Saturday was clear.

Two weeks without Diana sounded bleak. Gray.

He'd been right to worry that being with Diana was addicting. It would take some rescheduling, but they could see each other sooner than two weeks from now. If she was amenable, of course, to staying with him beyond tomorrow.

A firm date for the weekend after next would be best. Otherwise, she had a tendency to disappear when he turned his back. He'd had to track her down twice last night at the gala, and he'd had to catch her before she'd tiptoed out of his condo this morning. It would be good to know exactly when and where he'd see her again.

Diana bent to pick up a stick and flung it for the dog that had circled back to check on them. The sun that broke through the branches highlighted the red in her hair.

Quinn didn't want her to disappear. Forget setting one date. He should formalize their relationship. He'd had that conversation often enough in the past ten or so years. Women liked the security they got from a frank discussion of their relationship. As always, he'd make it clear that they were to be exclusive for as long as they were together. That they'd be together on weekends, and on weeknights when schedules permitted. That she was always welcome to spend the entire night, or he'd drive her back to her place. Her choice. Women always found it very generous of him to let them store some cosmetics at his place.

Patricia Cargill had opined on the very subject last summer, when they'd been thrown together for days on end, working with Texas Rescue and Relief on the Oklahoma border. Without electricity and cell service, people tended to talk. A lot.

Bethany Valrez made a point of letting everyone know that she keeps her things at your place.

Why would that be a topic of conversation?

Don't be obtuse. She's merely boasting that she's your girlfriend. I confess, I'm impressed that you let her keep a toothbrush at your place. For a commitment-phobic bachelor, it's really very generous of you. As your friend, though, I advise you to be careful. It could give some women the wrong impression.

I'm obviously not commitment-phobic, not when I've got one and only one woman keeping a toothbrush at my place.

For how long?

For as long as it makes sense for us to be together.

You are as romantic as a computer, Quinn MacDowell. Don't ever change.

He and Bethany had ended their relationship shortly after that, actually, although he couldn't recall why. Then his commitment to the hospital and his new appointment to the board had led to his year-long hiatus from dating. From women. From sex.

Diana ran a little way ahead, chasing a dog. Quinn watched her with a definitely male feeling of satisfaction. He'd ended a year's fast with a feast better than any he'd known. She would have been worth a five-year fast. Ten. She made him feel *that* good. He felt alive today, alive in every way.

The dog led Diana into the old graveyard. Quinn didn't miss the irony.

Diana came to an abrupt halt. The dog—Quinn did not know this one's name, although he was undoubtedly the descendent of an earlier blue heeler named Patch—barked at Diana, wanting her to play hide-and-seek among the tombstones. Quinn ruffled the top of the dog's head, feeling nostalgic because he recognized the black patch of fur over the dog's right eye and ear.

The memories came out of nowhere, crystal clear and bittersweet. Patch had been the ideal stable dog, herding the horses in from pasture at the same time every day, as if he'd had a perfectly working canine clock inside his brindled gray body. Quinn wanted to tell Diana about him, but when he looked at her face as she looked at the grave markers, he knew something was wrong.

"This is the ranch cemetery," he said, just to have something to say. It was a nondescript cluster of eight plain tombstones, none of them particularly old, only from the 1930s, and none of them particularly recent.

The newest one, he remembered from his boyhood explorations, was from 1957.

Diana ran her fingertips slowly, reverently, over the top of one tombstone. "I didn't know ranches had cemeteries."

"A lot do." He watched her run her fingers over a second tombstone as she walked in a slow grapevine between the graves. "If you worked and lived out here on all this land, it wouldn't make sense to be carted into town and buried in the city. That's what my dad told us."

"Oh." She lifted her finger immediately and turned to him. "Is your dad buried on your ranch?"

He shook his head. "No, he's in a cemetery near the hospital. He didn't want us to face the hassle of legal permits and bringing heavy equipment out here. That's why you don't see many graves on a ranch anymore."

She began moving down the second row. "These are all men's names. Only the years of their deaths." Diana was clearly upset, and she'd resumed her methodical touching of each tombstone.

Quinn wasn't sure what to say. Facts seemed safe. "They were ranch hands. Probably itinerant cowboys who would go from one ranch to another, looking for different kinds of work at different times of the year."

"Did these men work for your family?"

"No, my parents bought this ranch in 1980."

"So, no one knows anymore who Skip Laredo was? Where he was from?" She touched the marker, which bore only the date of death. "How old was he when he died?"

"I don't know, Diana."

Quinn had been around enough death to know that Diana was feeling that punch of grief. She'd gone from a sunny walk along a split-rail fence to grieving in a matter of minutes. It was the damnedest thing. It worried him.

He talked her through that punch. "The human body can't last indefinitely, but they may have lived a very long time. Death is a part of—"

He had to stop there. His usual logic didn't quite fit. Or maybe it did. "Death is part of many jobs. Ranching can be dangerous, but they must have loved it, to have worked on ranches until their last days."

His attempt at comfort backfired. Diana began crying tears, real tears, and they were definitely not a reaction to a perfect, beautiful moment. Quinn felt helpless. She was genuinely distressed at the thought of the men who'd been forgotten.

He'd never been with a woman so tenderhearted. No wine, no roses, no tasteful gold bracelet would soothe this kind of hurt. Quinn had none of those available, anyway. He had only himself. So, for what it was worth, he offered that to Diana. He touched her tentatively with one hand, and held his other arm open. "Would you like to cry on my shoulder, maybe?"

She turned into him. Without her high heels, she felt smaller, more vulnerable. He held her more tightly.

"I'm the last one of my family," she said, after a minute. She used the heel of one hand to wipe her cheeks, but he noticed she kept her other arm firmly around his waist. "The very last one."

Now her tears made sense. Quinn could handle discussions about mortality. He'd had dozens of patients ask him if they were going to die, and when. "You're afraid you'll be forgotten when you die. That is a painful thought."

Quinn felt a certain sense of relief at Diana's explanation. He took over the tear-wiping duties, using his thumb to smooth the wetness across her perfect cheek. The dry summer heat would evaporate the rest in no time. "I don't think you'll be the last of your family. Don't you see yourself being married someday, having children of your own?"

She shrugged. "I suppose. It could happen."

But, Quinn realized, she didn't really believe it would, although he couldn't imagine why she didn't. A woman like Diana Connor seemed cut out for motherhood. She was friendly, and beautiful to boot. Some man would get to know her well, become her husband, share her life.

Right now, he was the man who knew her. He was the one who knew what lay under her most superficial layers of sequins and smiles. But someday, it would be some other man, and that man would know her far better. He'd know what color her hair was in the frost as well as the sun. He'd know what she was like when she was round with pregnancy. He'd know what she was like when she was old.

Quinn felt a stab of envy for that unknown man.

He cleared his throat, heading into unfamiliar territory. "A matchmaker like you will find her own match. You will be married someday. You won't be forgotten when you pass away."

"It's not me I'm worried about. When that time comes, I won't care, will I? But I can't stand the thought that if I died tomorrow, no one would be left to know who my mother was. No one will visit her grave. She'll be just like these men. A name and a date. Nothing more."

Quinn was ready for fresh tears, but Diana stepped away from him and turned her face up to the branches of the shade tree. She flapped her hands in front of her cheeks and blinked her eyes a few times.

"I can't go back to the house so upset," she said. "It will just upset everyone else."

Quinn pictured his sisters-in-law. His mother. Jamie and Braden. "I think everyone could handle it, honestly."

"There's a quote my mother liked that I think is very true. 'There's enough misery in the world without you adding yours to it.' She wouldn't want me crying over her, not while I'm on a very nice date with a very nice man, and I don't want to be the guest that brings misery to your family picnic. Just give me a minute to get myself together."

She fluttered her hands with more determination. Quinn wished he could do more. He hated standing by helplessly, but no matter what poets or preachers said, pain couldn't be shared. When he'd been a kid and lost his grandmother, even his own mother's hugs could only do so much. He'd worked off a lot of his grief in the stables, shoveling out old hay, forking in new, with Patch as his constant companion.

Of course. Quinn whistled, hoping any of the dogs would come running. They all did. Within seconds, Diana couldn't keep fanning her face, because the dogs were licking her salty, wet hands. Her smile returned as she buried her hands in his dogs' ruffs, as she cooed "good boy" and found another stick to throw.

Quinn watched it all with a powerful, unfamiliar feeling in his chest. As a cardiologist, he knew emotions couldn't affect the size of the heart, but if he were less educated, if he'd lived in a long-ago, superstitious century, he might say his heart swelled as he watched Diana Connor playing with Patch the Second.

Chapter Nine

They arrived back at the house after the food had already been blessed and the potato salad passed. They washed up and took their places at the picnic table on the flagstone back porch.

Diana bore no resemblance to the woman who'd mourned the forgotten ranch hands. Quinn supposed a backyard cookout was the same as a party, and Diana was in her element, sparkling and happy. Her joy in the meal was infectious, and Quinn watched his whole family benefit from Diana being at their table.

She knew Lana well enough to encourage her to recount her tales of the bridal worries she'd experienced the day before her wedding. Quinn hadn't had any idea that Lana, the coolly competent director of research and development at West Central Texas Hospital, had worried about such frivolous things as the width of ribbons.

Lana couldn't seem to believe how stressed out she'd been over it herself. Her obsession seemed normal and amusing, though, once Diana shared stories of other brides she'd known.

Diana was a dream guest to have at a gathering, the one who made everyone feel at ease, even when the guests were family who'd known each other their entire lives. His mother had caught his eye several times and directed all sorts of approving pantomimes at him.

He ate brisket, he laughed with everyone else and he watched Diana. As he had at the gala, Quinn wondered what was behind Diana's magic. Trained to pay attention to details, he started to notice a pattern.

Diana brought out the best in everyone by finding out what they needed in order to relax and be themselves. Last night, he'd needed to stop his self-imposed no-play-and-all-work policy, now that the hospital was going to survive the damage done by its former CEO. Becky Cargill had needed to be able to literally let go of her loose dress and dance. Quinn never would have guessed that Lana needed to be able to laugh at her temporary wedding madness. If anyone stayed in Diana's vicinity long enough, she'd find a way to make him or her feel better about themselves.

So that's how she does it. Her "magic" could be analyzed and elucidated, which made him respect her abilities all the more. Even when meeting strangers, she had an uncanny instinct about what people needed. When baby Sammy was passed to Diana for some time in her lap, his mother Kendry had no more than glanced at the red sunglasses perched on Diana's head before Diana had taken them off and set them out of the baby's sight. Kendry sat back to talk to her husband, and only then did Quinn realize that she'd been poised on the edge of her seat, ready to intervene if Sammy should make a grab for those red glasses.

Diana was a keen observer, and she used that skill to please others. But when it came to Diana, who observed her? Who found out what she needed? She made it impossible by appearing to have no cares of her own.

The meal was over and everyone was lingering over brownies when Quinn's mother asked Diana what she'd seen on her walk. Diana had given a charming answer, one that segued naturally into encouraging his mother to talk about her pride and joy, her flower beds.

"We stopped at the old cemetery," Quinn said, as Diana was setting down her iced tea.

Quinn doubted anyone but he noticed the way Diana's tea glass slipped a mere quarter of an inch, plunking down on the wooden plank of the table just hard enough to make the ice rattle. He didn't want to upset her, but deep down, he knew—he was the only one who knew—that she was torn up at the thought of her own mother being as forgotten as the buried ranch hands. Maybe he could fix it for her. His mother knew everything there was to know about this land.

"Did those men work the River Mack, Mom?"

"No, that cemetery is part of the hundred and forty we bought from Whitey McCormick. May I give Sam his bottle, Kendry?"

Diana kept her face turned away from Quinn.

Aw, hell. His mother didn't know anything about the men in those graves. Quinn cursed himself for dimming Diana's bright smile. He didn't have her instincts, obviously. He'd thought surely his mother would know all about the cemetery.

Once Quinn's mother had her grandson happily settled in her arms, however, she picked up the subject again. "It was 1990, right after Christmas. Whitey came over here out of the blue and offered to sell it to us. He said he wanted a real family to take over his land, not a conglomerate."

"The Watersons are on the east side," Braden said. "They're a real family."

Marion MacDowell looked around the table at Quinn and his brothers. "You children were so cute, I think you sealed the deal for us before we knew the land was even for sale."

Jamie laughed at that. "I'll bet Mrs. Waterson thought Luke and Jimmy were cuter."

"Well, there were three of you and only two of them, so we had the advantage. Do you remember Whitey?"

Jamie was watching his son drink. "I was only three years old, Mom. Make sure Sam doesn't get too much air with that bottle."

"I know how to give a baby a bottle, young man."

Diana sighed a little. Quinn wanted to believe it was a sound of contentment, but he couldn't lie to himself. Diana's sigh had been wistful. Full of longing. Lonely.

Diana was relieved the conversation was turning away from the cemetery. She'd been having such a good time at this family party, she didn't want to think about the poor dead cowboys. She wanted to keep living the little fantasy in her head, the one she'd kept up the whole meal, the one where Marion MacDowell was her mother.

She wouldn't take for granted her mother's potato salad. Even if she'd eaten it every day of her twenty-seven years, Diana would still tell her mother how wonderful it was. She would already know the recipe by heart, of course. It was apparent from the conversation that Marion had a health problem that brought unpredictable bad days, so Diana would have insisted her mother take it easy. She would have come early today and made the potato salad for her. She and her mother would have been very close.

"I remember Whitey McCormack," Quinn said.

Diana hoped her smile didn't slip. Did Quinn have to intrude on her little fantasy? Did he have to remind her about cemeteries, about her real mother's location?

"I remember him, too," Braden said. "Whitey was old as the hills, with a long white beard."

This seemed only to encourage Quinn. "Yes, and he always carried a staff that was taller than he was, and you'll like this part, Diana. He had a great dog."

Braden took another brownie from the serving platter. "I remember that dog. Little scrappy thing. Runt of the litter. I swear, the way Whitey bragged about the runt, I assumed it was a positive word until I was in high school. Being a runt had to be a great thing. Who wouldn't want to be a runt? I was sad when Dad explained that I wasn't the runt."

"Sure you were," Jamie said, with a touch of irritation to his voice.

Diana thought Braden was going on a bit too long about runts, too. Quinn was getting those crinkles at the corners of his eyes again, the good ones that meant he might break into a smile at any moment.

Braden kept singing the praises of runts. "When I called someone 'runt,' it was a compliment of the highest order."

"You can shut up anytime now." Jamie grabbed a

beer from the cooler the brothers had set conveniently in reach and opened the bottle by hitting the cap just so on the edge of the picnic table.

"Anything you say, runt."

Then Quinn and Braden and their mother—and even Jamie—all laughed, and Diana knew it was a family joke. It was so easy to fall right back into her fantasy of being in this family.

Sam fussed, and Jamie stood up to take him from Marion. Braden stood, too, and Diana noticed the "runt" was actually a tiny bit taller than his oldest brother. Braden was closest to Marion, so Sammy was passed from Marion to Braden to Jamie to Kendry, who excused herself, saying it was nap time and she'd have Sammy asleep in a jiffy.

In the brief silence that followed the baby's crying and the brothers' ribbing about runts, Marion turned toward Diana. "I'm sorry I couldn't tell you more about the cemetery."

"Please, don't worry about it for a second."

"It made her sad," Quinn said, "because no one remembers the men buried there."

Diana was appalled. She didn't want Marion to think anything about her picnic had been anything less than a success. Her smile wobbled. She couldn't help it. How could Quinn do this to her?

"Cemeteries aren't exactly happy places," Marion said.

Diana couldn't keep smiling when Marion said the subject wasn't happy, so she took a sip of tea.

"You have a sensitive heart, I can tell, for you to worry about men long gone," Marion said.

Diana was at a loss. She didn't know how to handle

this topic at a party, so she kept drinking tea like a fool, looking over the rim of her glass at the others. Braden, Jamie and Lana all looked interested, but not upset. They didn't seem to think the picnic was ruined. Diana didn't trust herself to look at Quinn. She wanted to smack him for bringing up the subject.

Marion was watching her as she set her tea down. "I sure hate for you to leave here sad about it. Maybe you can think of it this way. Whitey knew every one of those men buried on his land. They had to have touched him in some way, and changed him, and made him the man he was. It might have been something as silly as telling him a joke that made him laugh, but every one of those men touched Whitey.

"My boys knew Whitey, and he made an impression on them. Well, Jamie was too young, but Braden and Quinn knew Whitey, and then they in turn made an impression on Jamie, and now he has a boy of his own. So you see, those cowboys' lives might not be remembered in detail, but they touched people, and those people touched other people, generation after generation. People don't walk this earth for no reason."

As she kept her hand on her cold tea glass, Diana felt Quinn squeeze her other hand under the table. She kept her attention on his mother's kind face. "Oh, that's something my mother would have said. That every experience touches us and makes us who we are in some small way."

"Well, there you have it. Jamie, refill her tea." Marion smiled at Diana, looking every inch the calm, wise and beautiful image of motherhood. "So tell me, dear, how has Quinn touched you?"

Quinn and Braden and Jamie, all three of them, exchanged a look. The silence lasted a heartbeat, and then the men simultaneously began coughing and choking and snickering.

"Yes," Braden gasped, "tell us how Quinn has touched you."

The Madonna-like Marion rolled her eyes and threw up a hand in disgust.

"Oh, grow up, gentlemen. Try to move past age twelve." But her expression wasn't as stern as her words, and Diana found herself on the verge of laughing, too, if only to laugh at the way the MacDowell men were laughing. They were doctors, for goodness' sake. She expected more from them—which made it even funnier that they were cracking up in such a juvenile way.

Marion smacked Quinn's arm—*he deserved that*—to make him sit back, so she could reach across him and place her hand over Diana's arm, where it rested on the table as her fingertips grew numb on the frosty glass. "Ignore them. I'm hoping there's at least one positive thing you've gotten from knowing my Quinn."

"I've only known him for a day," Diana began apologetically.

This seemed to silence everyone's sniggering. She felt Marion's hand jerk a little bit.

Diana bit her lip and looked around the table.

Kendry came back. "Did I miss anything?"

Marion let go of Diana's arm. "Quinn and Diana have only been together one day. I never would have guessed." She sounded astonished. Perhaps girlfriends of only a day weren't supposed to come to family picnics. Diana hoped desperately that Marion couldn't tell that she'd slept with her son already.

It was definitely time to put this party back on track.

She was willing to be the clown to do it. Everyone loved dopey, bubbly Diana.

"We met last night, at the hospital gala." Diana smiled too brightly. Even she could feel it. "If you count that as our first date, then this is really the second. Two days. We've known each other twice as long as I said. I'm so bad at math. But already, he's ruined me for champagne. I liked the cheap stuff just fine, until he gave me real champagne. Now I'll never look at sparkling wine the same way again. Isn't that terrible?"

She let go of her iced tea and twisted quickly to place the icy wetness on her fingertips on the back of Quinn's neck, like she imagined an annoying little sister should. He yelped and jumped in surprise, and everyone laughed.

Braden stood and tapped his beer bottle with a spoon, directing everyone's attention to himself—and preventing Quinn from retaliating. "Speaking of champagne, Lana and I brought the good stuff. We have an announcement to make. We're going to have a baby. We're due the first week of November."

The news was wonderful. Everyone stood to hug each other, and while the champagne cork was being popped, Lana whispered in Diana's ear, "Since we just got married two weeks ago, I'd appreciate it if you didn't do the math. It's a little embarrassing. We jumped the gun."

"I don't think anyone cares," Diana said immediately, not wanting Lana to feel badly for a moment.

"You're right. It doesn't matter how long we've been together." Lana kissed Diana on the cheek and turned to hug Kendry.

Diana wondered, just for a moment, if Lana had been trying to put *her* at ease.

She hadn't meant to make anyone worry about her. Just the opposite. Still, it was a nice idea, that first Marion and then Lana had cared about her feelings.

Quinn apparently wasn't averse to pointing out the obvious when it came to his brother. "Let's see. First week of November means you got busy around Valentine's Day. Very nice."

"Valentine's Day," Jamie agreed. "Wasn't that the weekend you skipped out on your job to go camping? In the winter? No sane person would do that. It must have been cold in that tent."

"You're a pair of geniuses," Braden said. "I couldn't have done the math without you."

Chapter Ten

They were supposed to go out for dinner and dancing.

During the entire hour-long drive back to Austin, Quinn had strategized their plans for the evening. Diana knew all the good DJs in town, and she checked her phone to see who was playing where that night. They agreed to stop first at Quinn's so he could get fresh clothes, then to go to her house so she could change for a night out. Before going to any nightclubs, they'd have dinner at a café Quinn liked. It was a solid plan, agreeable to both.

They made it as far as the elevator in Quinn's building. Again.

This time, when he carried her through the door, they only made it to the leather sofa. Afterward, they made it to the shower. Eventually, they'd made it to the phone to order some pizza, which they'd ended up eating in front of the fireplace.

"The air-conditioning is on," Diana had protested. "It's June."

"You want a fire, you get a fire."

She'd declared if they were going to do something so silly, they should do it right, and she'd turned off every light in the place. She'd even placed a throw pillow over the glowing lights that remained on the satellite box when the television was off. While the moon lingered outside his balcony, they'd eaten pizza in his living room, staring at the fire.

At the cityscape beyond his panoramic windows.

At each other.

It had been spectacularly beautiful. He'd opened a red wine that he'd been saving for a special occasion, something he'd described as spicy and floral and hard to find. She'd worn his shirt, he'd worn none, and she'd known it was yet another perfect moment with Quinn MacDowell. She'd made sure he didn't see her tears.

The entire time, Diana had not looked at a clock. Sunday would come soon enough, and her weekend would be over.

When she woke, it was to full daylight. Sunday was here.

She rolled over to face Quinn, who was sound asleep on his stomach, his face turned away from her. He slept in the nude, warm golden skin against cool white sheets. Diana reached out to toy with a piece of his hair. It was a luxury, sheer luxury, to be able to touch him just because she felt like it. She ran her finger over his shoulder, feeling the muscle relaxed in his deep sleep, the same muscle that had flexed as he held his body over hers last night.

She'd worn him out, she thought with a smile. That

was an achievement she could look back on—privately. Very privately.

I'll look back...and remember...and miss what I had...

She let her hand trail down his body, resting her palm on the large muscle of his backside, very lightly, so she wouldn't wake him. This was her moment to appreciate the beauty of a man. When he woke, would they have sex again? Would it start playfully, would it end hungrily?

It would end. That was the important thing.

Diana snatched her hand back, sudden fear making her heart feel like ice in her chest. She had to stop making memories now. This minute.

Someday, she would lie next to another man, maybe even the husband Quinn saw in her future. She'd watch him sleeping, and she'd remember Quinn, and she'd picture this moment in her memory. It would be hard to bear.

She'd made too many memories. It was time to go.

She'd say goodbye, though. Quinn had said yesterday that no one sneaked out after a night like they'd had. Well, they'd had another wonderful night, so she'd say goodbye before she left him here, in this well-designed, exclusive living space that fit him to a T.

She was just about to slip out of bed when his phone rang, jarringly. With a grunt, Quinn grabbed his phone from the nightstand and rolled over. She watched him open one eye to look at the screen before answering.

"MacDowell."

A long pause followed. While he listened, he looked at her, smiled that half smile, then scrubbed his face with one hand. "Right," he said to the caller, in a clipped tone she hadn't heard before. "That's a dihydropyridine available in Europe. It didn't cause the bradycardia."

Ah, doctor-ly stuff. She slipped out of bed quietly and put his bathrobe on as quickly as she could. He made a grab for the edge of the robe while giving medical orders to the caller in a confident, almost cocky, tone. It was sexy in a man-in-charge way, she had to admit, but she dodged his hand and headed for the bathroom in the hall, where she wouldn't disturb his call.

She scooped up her clothes from the day before, wrinkling her nose at their wrinkled state. She'd have to leave the building in the same outfit she'd been wearing the day before. Quinn had a high-tech washer and dryer in an alcove in the hallway that could probably accomplish the same task as the local Laundromat in half the time. Her red denim shorts would have to be worn as they were, but she could wash her underwear, bra and white shirt together. Diana started the two-minute quick wash setting before bringing her purse into the bathroom.

She had her normal-sized purse with her, which meant she had a hairbrush and the disposable finger-tip toothbrushes she used at work when lunch had been too much of an Austin fiesta. She decided to use the cosmetics in her purse, too. She wanted her last impression to be as good as possible. She wanted Quinn to remember her at her best, as selfish as that was.

Sunday had come so soon.

She heard water running in the master suite. His cell phone rang again, and the indistinct rumble of his voice once more had the distinct edge of a doctor to it.

She dug her own cell phone out of her purse. Maybe her friends had missed her this weekend. Maybe she had a couple of text messages to return, an invite to a Sunday afternoon get-together that would ease her back to her regular life.

Her phone battery had died.

Look at the bright side. When you charge it, you might find a half-dozen invites.

She hoped so. She was going to need something to do this afternoon, something to distract her. There was always the animal shelter. She could make other people happy there.

She left the bathroom, transferred her clothes to the dryer and headed for the kitchen. Quinn was at the stove, stopping her heart in blue jeans and bare feet, wearing a navy blue T-shirt that hugged his chest the way she wanted to. He was cooking eggs with his cell phone wedged between his ear and shoulder, but he put the spatula down to scribble something on a notepad.

Resigned, Diana took a seat at one of his bar stools. It looked like she was going to make one more memory: a handsome man cooking breakfast for her. That was another first. Darn it.

This farewell was going to suck.

Quinn hung up his call and had placed another, dialing the numbers he'd written on the notepad, when he noticed her sitting there. He did a double take, and raised an eyebrow as he checked her out with the phone held up to his ear.

"You're all cleaned up. Did you want to go out for breakfast?"

"No, thanks. Looks like you've got it under—"

He held up his finger in the standard "one minute" gesture as whomever he'd called apparently picked up. He started rattling off information that was obviously routine for him. "MacDowell, Quinn, license M nineteen eighty-nine, patient Norma Gildart, date of birth—" He paused to read the date off his notepad. "Amlodipine ten milligrams QD number seven. No refills. Instruct patient to follow up ASAP." He disconnected his call with one hand and lifted the skillet off the burner with the other.

"Sorry," he said. "Brian had asked if he could transfer the answering service over to me this morning. I said yes before I knew you. He'll pick it back up around seven."

"Oh. Well, I was saying that it's very nice of you to cook eggs for me." But Quinn's phone had started to ring when she'd started her sentence, and he gave her an apologetic smile as he took the call.

He tucked the phone between his ear and shoulder again as he opened a cabinet and took out a dinner plate, then another, then shook the eggs onto them. Diana silently got off her bar stool and found forks in the third drawer she tried. She got another apologetic smile for her effort.

She was done eating, and she was certain his eggs were cold, by the time he hung up. The lack of intimacy was welcome, in its way, considering she'd be leaving once her clothes were dry.

"What would you like to do today?" Quinn asked. "I have to be attached to this phone, but we could still go somewhere like a park, somewhere I can answer when it rings."

It was going to be up to her, then, to declare the weekend officially over. She sighed, and doodled on her plate with her fork, and tried not to get sentimental over the kindness of being served scrambled eggs.

And then Quinn stood over her where she perched, and he kissed her, his lips warm and soft, with one hand cradling the back of her head.

She placed her palm on the soft navy cotton of his T-shirt. On his chest muscle. On his heart.

Don't forget me.

"I have to be going," she said. "It's been a great weekend, but I have to be going."

"Don't go. The phone won't ring this often all day. It comes in clusters."

Diana wondered if Quinn really thought she was leaving because of a few phone calls. She slid off the bar stool, but he didn't let go of her.

"Unless it's the answering service, I have to answer. I can let the answering service go to voice mail, as long as I call them back within ten minutes." He moved his hand from the back of her head slowly down, down to her lower back, where he pulled her close to him, body to body, bathrobe to jeans. Her bare toes brushed the inside arch of his foot. "It won't be the Sunday I'd had in mind. A badly timed call can make something turn into a ten-minute quickie when I'd rather spend an hour."

She turned her face away. He did expect her to stay for the rest of Sunday, to make love, fast or slow. She could not. Her emotions were all caught up in the sex. They had been from the first. When he whispered to her how beautiful she was, how perfect, how right, her heart kept thinking he meant her. All of her, not just her body.

"But we can make the best of it. Diana? Look at me."

She smiled first, then turned back to him with the proper expression on her face. Friendly. No regrets. "I really have to be going. It's Sunday, and we said we'd stay together until Sunday."

He did not move a muscle. Not an inch. Not for an eternity.

His phone rang. He glared at it, but he answered it, and as she backed up, he glared at her, too, and caught her with a hand at her waist. The moment he hung up, he tossed the phone on the counter and put his other hand on her waist. "I hope you're not going to hold me to that agreement. I want to see you again."

"You do?" She tried to be cautious, but she could feel the hope expanding in her chest almost painfully.

"Yes. Without a doubt."

She had doubts. They didn't move in the same circles. They had no friends in common. Their incomes were hugely unequal, their level of education, as well. They hadn't discussed their lives, where they saw themselves five years from now. Ten.

Quinn kissed her, softly at first, then with increasing intimacy, a slide of tongues that began as a slow exploration of texture, but quickly turned harder, more demanding. Her tongue answered, her body answered, and his hands gripped her waist more tightly. He lifted her onto the bar stool. Her robe fell open over her lap as his warm hand pressed her knee outward, and she felt the roughness of denim on her inner thighs as Quinn closed the space between their bodies.

"Diana, beautiful Diana, how could you doubt that I'd want to see you again? I need more of you, more of this."

This. This, that was coming to mean so much. This, that meant more every time.

"You and me, together," he said, raining hard, quick kisses across her cheeks, her nose. "I want to know you better, to be with you, to be a couple."

She brought her arms over his shoulders and buried both hands in his hair, tugging his head to angle him for a deeper kiss.

The phone rang. Quinn made a sound of frustration against her mouth, then turned his head to answer while keeping her entire body pressed against his. She rained soft kisses on his throat while he barked "MacDowell" into the phone and started listening. This close, Diana could hear the caller, as well. A man's voice, speaking in medical terms, sounded very young as he tripped over his words.

"Slow down," Quinn ordered. He listened a few more moments. "For God's sake, if she's coding, then hang the hell up. If she's not, then report this right. Give me the presenting symptoms."

Diana eased away from Quinn, leaning back in the bar stool. Quinn turned toward the high countertop and leaned one arm on it, dropping his head and listening intently. He started outlining steps for the caller to take, Diana could tell that much, although he might as well have been speaking a foreign language. It was all Greek to her. Or Latin. Didn't doctors speak in Latin terms?

She tried to make herself laugh, but the truth was, this was horrifying. Somewhere, a woman was in trouble, and Quinn was telling a younger doctor what to do about it. He had the caller repeat back his orders, twice, and then Quinn asked for a Dr. Gregory.

During the pause that followed, a full minute at the least, she studied Quinn. He was motionless, every muscle in his body taut with tension, listening intently. He was dealing with death, she thought, and the nausea was unexpected. She put her fingers to her lips and breathed deeply.

"Gregory. It's Quinn. You know what I'm going to say. Who the hell is that?" He paused again, then nodded at the answer. "I agree. Get him out of there. He can't keep a cool head to save his own life, let alone anyone else's."

Moments later, he hung up and set his phone down,

then scrubbed both hands over his face for a moment, as if he'd rub his razor stubble away. Then he turned to Diana. "Okay. Where were we?"

She swallowed, more unsure than ever that she was the right match for this man. Would she be able to soothe that kind of tension away for him, day after day, when it affected her worse than it did him? If they were going to be a couple, she had to try.

"Are you okay?" she asked.

"Fine. That was just a first-year idiot. When doctors graduate and start working for real, you find out quickly who can hang and who can't."

"But…are *you* okay?"

"I'm fine." He looked at her closely. "I think the question is, are you okay?"

She took a breath, but it wasn't very deep. Her chest felt tight. "I'm worried about that woman. And that poor doctor—he's going to get fired, isn't he? You're acting like that call was nothing, but you were very intense a minute ago."

He cocked his head a little, studying her, and then he began to grin. "You are the most tenderhearted person I've ever known."

Diana felt a little insulted. A little hot inside, irritated that he'd be amused at her.

He took her hands in his and gave them a shake. "Don't worry. That woman is going to be fine. Her condition is very treatable, and I was listening to the nurses in the background. They weren't letting that first-year screw it up. He's not cut out for the E.R., plain and simple. He may still be a good doctor someday. Maybe he'll have an eagle eye for pinpoints on film and become a stellar radiologist. You never know. But it's his job to find where he fits in. It's my job to make sure he does no harm in the meantime, so he's out of my hospital."

He gave her hands a deliberate kind of shake, one that made her arms shake, too, and her shoulder muscles loosen up, all in one expert move. "I'm used to this. I'm trained for it. You're not, so it may have seemed like a big deal to you. Trust me when I say I'm okay."

It made sense, when he spelled it out that way. She was glad to hear that the woman would survive—and the young doctor, in a way. "You don't see this as being a problem for us as a couple? Me being stressed out by your job?"

"No. It may never happen again. I don't normally try to see anyone on days I have call. Of course, if you go home now, then I won't get another call for hours. Murphy's Law. But if you want to leave, we could see each other after seven."

"You don't normally see anyone when you have call? You've got a system for this when it comes to girlfriends?"

Quinn's grin faded. "I've been a doctor for years, so yes, I've had girlfriends in this situation. Trying to be together on call days doesn't work."

"It didn't work with them. What about with me?" Diana thought her heart would pound out of her chest. She didn't want to know about past women. She was unique. Beautiful, perfect, right—Quinn had said so. How could she only be right for days when he wasn't on call?

"You deserve all my attention, not these constant interruptions."

That was a rehearsed line if she'd ever heard one. The disappointment was sharp.

Quinn sat on his bar stool once more. He began flipping through his phone screens. "Not this Saturday, but next, I've got the whole day free. I want to spend it with you."

When she said nothing, he asked, "Do you want to spend it with me?"

He sounded just uncertain enough for her to answer him. "Of course I do." Her words came out as a whisper around the lump in her throat. He wanted to see her again in two weeks, when he wasn't on call.

That was not the same thing as being a couple. When a man needed a woman, when he wanted to know her better, he didn't wait two weeks to see her.

"Excellent." Quinn sounded relieved. Happy, even. He leaned forward on his bar stool and kissed her on the cheek.

"Did you have any other dates in mind?" She was amazed at her own ability to be a smart aleck.

"I think I can rearrange some obligations this Friday."

She must be lousy at sarcasm. He was taking her seriously.

"You should bring some things to keep here, so you can spend the night without having to pack every time. You know, a toothbrush, makeup, extra clothes, whatever you want."

"We wouldn't stay at my house? Is it more convenient for you here?"

"Your house is cute. You'll let me keep a razor there, won't you?" He grinned again, a man pleased with himself.

"And when your schedule does not permit us to get together? I assume we don't see anyone else in between these dates."

Ah, that wiped the smile off his face.

"This would be an exclusive arrangement. Very. That won't be a problem for you, will it?"

She felt her cheeks grow hot. The nausea returned, but for an entirely different reason. She looked him in his green, green eyes for the first time since he'd started laying out his plans for their future. "I'm usually so busy with my one-night stands, it might be hard to break that habit."

He didn't miss her sarcasm this time. "I meant, you're not involved with anyone else, are you?"

She gasped. "Would I have slept with you this weekend if I already had a boyfriend?"

For just a fraction of a second, he hesitated. Just a moment where she knew he'd thought that yes, some people would have a weekend fling on the side.

Not her. Never her. He didn't know her at all.

Diana wanted to leave, immediately. Quinn was ruining every perfect memory she'd made.

His phone rang. He glanced at the screen and punched it with one finger, silencing it. "It was the service. Now I've got ten minutes. Let me start by apologizing. That was a stupid question. I'm sorry."

"Thank you," she said, but her lips felt stiff and the words were forced. She jumped off the bar stool and spun toward the hallway.

"C'mon, Diana. I'm distracted with these calls right now. You can see how crazy it gets. That's why it would be better to see each other on the weekends I'm off."

"So, basically, you are asking if I'm willing to schedule booty calls on an ongoing basis."

"Booty calls?" The expression of disbelief on his face

said it all. "For God's sake, I don't think in those terms. It's called dating. Dinners. Movies. Whatever you like."

He could call it whatever he liked. Putting it in sophisticated terms didn't change what it was.

She headed for the dryer. She wanted her clothes, and she wanted to get out of there while she was still furious. Tears could come later, in privacy.

Quinn followed her. "What is so awful about asking you out for a date this Friday?"

Diana opened the dryer. She reached her hand into the hot, steamy interior. Swell. Her clothes were still damp. She pulled her underwear out, anyway, and tugged it on under the bathrobe.

"What are you doing? You're getting very dramatic over this."

"Let me make sure I have this straight," she said, grabbing her red shorts off the top of the washing machine where she'd left them. She wriggled them over the wet underwear. "I get a toothbrush, a little drawer space and great sex when your schedule allows. Oh— and dinners out. I assume when you have official shindigs, I get to dress up and be your arm candy. Did I miss anything?"

She dropped the bathrobe to the floor. Let Quinn get an eyeful while she put on her wet bra. It soothed her pride to see him distracted by what he'd never have again. She whipped her shirt right-side-out, and put it on, too.

She buttoned as fast as she could. "That arm candy thing would be a challenge. I don't do elegant well."

She marched down the hall to retrieve her white sneakers from under the couch.

"Diana!" He caught her around the waist, then let go. "Your clothes are wet. Jeez."

With her shoes dangling from her fingers, she slung her purse over her shoulder and headed for the door.

He easily matched her strides. "It's ridiculous to leave in wet clothes. What's wrong with scheduling a date next Friday?"

She turned to face him with her sneakers in one hand, the doorknob gripped in the other. "Nothing, when you put it like that, with all your cool reasoning. But you got my hopes up when you said we'd be a couple.

"What if you're on call, and a phone call does upset you? Will you wait two weeks to talk about it with me? See—that never occurred to you. That's what I think a girlfriend should be. A friend. One who is around, not one who is scheduled for dinner and bed at a convenient time later in the week. What happens if I miss you on a Wednesday?"

"We have phones, you know. I'm home most nights after seven, if you'd like to call."

"Wow," Diana said, a little stunned at his honesty. She could be honest, too. "That's even more horrible than I thought. Remember that woman in the red dress? You'll see her at another big event. Ask her to dance. She'll be a good match for you. I am not."

With that, she executed another first: a grand exit, complete with the perfect slamming of the door.

Chapter Eleven

It had never occurred to Diana that a grand exit would be difficult when the guy was rich.

If the rich guy lived in a high-rise building that had an elevator, then while one waited for the elevator, the rich guy could easily stroll to the elevator bank and continue the conversation.

Darn it all.

"You've made your point," Quinn said, sounding like a stern parent from TV. "Come inside."

There were three sets of elevator doors. Diana stood in front of the one that sounded like machinery was running behind it. *Hurry up, hurry up.*

She refused to look at Quinn. She'd had her say, and she needed to stay mad for a while, at least long enough to get a taxi and get home. Lord, how long would it take for a taxi? They were pretty scarce in Austin. She might need to walk to Sixth Street to hail one.

She started to pull on one sneaker, balancing with her hand on the call button, with its arrow-pointing-down emblem. Although it was already lit, she pushed it again, anyway. *Hurry, hurry.*

One of the other condo doors in the hallway opened, and a neighbor stepped out to get his Sunday paper. "Morning, Quinn."

"Good morning," he answered, and Diana credited his unflappable manners to Marion MacDowell. She felt another pang—she'd probably never see her pretend-mother again.

The neighbor looked at her, and made no move to take his paper and go.

Quinn reached for her arm, but she warded him off with her sneaker. "Leave me alone. We've said everything there is to say."

"You're making a scene," he said through clenched teeth.

"I'm putting on a sneaker." She put her foot down and started on the second sneaker. The interested neighbor was not her problem. "You shouldn't have followed me out here. You're ruining it."

He kept his voice low, but it was seething with displeasure. "I'm ruining your attempt to run away again?"

The warmth of the dryer had left her clothes, but not the dampness. The air-conditioning in the hallway was close to making her shiver. "We're not a match. I should have left after our last dance at the gala. None of this weekend was supposed to happen."

"Ah, that last dance. That beautiful moment that will never come again. You're damned right it won't, not if you leave. Nothing can happen if you leave."

The elevator was almost to their floor. She could hear

it. It was time for the second grand exit of her life. She'd make this one kinder.

"I stayed, and we had a perfect weekend, Quinn, full of wonderful moments. I'll never forget it. Thank you."

Diana pressed a last kiss to his lips.

The elevator didn't stop. She heard it travel past them, up to a higher floor.

They stood there, staring at each other.

Quinn opened his mouth to say something, but Diana put her hand up to stop him. "Shh. We said goodbye."

She bounced on her toes a little, just to keep moving and stay warm, as they waited some more. Finally, the elevator arrived—not the one she was standing in front of. The next one over.

She kept her chin up as she walked three steps to her left.

"Goodbye, Quinn."

But as she turned to go in, another person was coming out, a taller woman, ready for an elegant Sunday brunch in slacks and pearls. Diana remembered her from the gala: Becky's stepsister, Quinn's friend in the stunning blue gown.

Patricia Cargill barely glanced at Diana as she walked into the hallway.

Diana stepped into the elevator. She closed her eyes, unable to bear the reflections of herself in the mirrors. The doors slid shut, but not before she heard Patricia's voice, as refined as Patricia herself.

"Hello, Quinn. Did I catch you coming out to get your paper? What perfect timing. It's like you were waiting for me."

* * *

Quinn resented the clock. As he let Patricia into his condo, his phone rang, flashing the time at him before he could swipe the screen to answer. It wasn't even noon. They'd agreed to be together on Sunday, but Diana had left when they still could have made love for hours.

What would have been the purpose of those extra hours in bed, before they'd go their separate ways? Sex just for physical pleasure?

A booty call.

"MacDowell," he snapped into the phone. It was the answering service, calling back because it had been ten minutes since he'd missed their last call.

Ten freaking minutes since he'd explained to Diana that he wanted a long-term, exclusive relationship with her.

Ten minutes since she'd told him his offer was ruining her idea of a perfect weekend. That made no sense. She'd shushed him, *shushed* him, and gotten on the elevator and left.

Unbelievable.

The answering service relayed five messages to him, each one nonurgent, nothing that the patients couldn't have called his nurses about on Monday. For this, he'd lost his concentration on what Diana was saying. He'd botched something up—he remembered apologizing—oh, yeah. The exclusive thing.

Patricia was helping herself to his kitchen, loading a K-Cup into his coffee machine. He watched her select a coffee mug from his cabinet, as if it mattered which drug logo freebie she was seen using. He was the only one here to see her, anyway. That was Tricia, though, fastidious to a fault. He knew her well, two years to Diana's two days.

Yet he'd known Diana well enough to know she didn't have a boyfriend. She wasn't using him to cheat on someone else. It was impossible to imagine her sneaking in a weekend fling while her regular guy was out of town. Why the hell had he said something so stupid?

He remembered an important detail: she'd already been upset before that. She didn't like that he'd developed a routine with other girlfriends while he was on call. What had she expected? He couldn't go back and undo his past.

He sat on the bar stool, feeling like gravity was too much to fight standing up. He'd give a million dollars to feel as good as he had this time yesterday. A million dollars.

Tricia slid the coffee mug under his nose. "You need this more than I do. Rough night at the hospital?"

"Fishing for info is beneath you. I know you've noticed that there are two plates here."

She laughed. "I was trying to be nice. I take it whoever she is has left the building, and I'm not in danger of getting an eyeful of any supermodel strolling around in her all-together?"

"You saw her go."

Quinn sipped the coffee. Maybe it would clear his mind, which was currently short-circuiting after the exit that Diana had made.

"That girl? I assumed she was your neighbor's little hottie. A fruity sequined shirt— Oh, Quinn." She chuckled. "Wherever did you find her?"

Quinn shot her a look, one that would have silenced

any man who insulted a woman he was with. *Had been* with. Past tense.

Patricia abruptly stopped laughing, but not from his look. She'd apparently just remembered who Diana was. "Wait—not the real estate agent from the gala?"

Quinn didn't bother answering her. He wanted to mentally review the whole disastrous last scene with Diana, pull out the details and find the precise moment it had all gone sour.

His uninvited visitor wasn't helping any. Patricia cleared away the plates and forks and put the dirty skillet in the sink, turning on the water with a quick flick of her wrist, rinsing traces that Diana had been there down the drain.

"Is there a point to this visit?" he asked. He could hear the irritation in his own voice.

So, apparently, could Patricia. "Don't take your lousy sex life out on the woman who gives you coffee."

"It wasn't lousy," he said.

She snapped the water off.

"And you can't give me coffee I already own." He took another sip after his halfhearted dig. He and Patricia had gone from acquaintances to friends since last year's relief trip, but Quinn couldn't enjoy their usual sparring today.

Patricia dried her hands and came to lean on the counter next to him. "Let's go out. I'll buy you coffee. I wanted to bounce some ideas off you about Texas Rescue. I got quite the scoop out of Karen Weaver on Friday."

"Who?"

"The new director. Honestly, Quinn, you spoke with her at length during the gala. Where's that famous head for details?" She gave his head a little push to the side with the tips of her fingers, then smoothed down the hair she couldn't really have messed up.

Diana's fingers had been in his hair just ten minutes ago. No, more like twenty now. Quinn jerked away from Patricia's hand, then pushed his own hand through his hair, trying to play off the fact that he was overreacting to everything.

"I can't go out. I'm on call."

"What's new? Bring your phone."

"Not today. I'll take a rain check."

"Karen will be at our steering committee meeting." Patricia pouted and tugged him out of his chair. "Come eat with me. I can't exactly talk about her when she's right there."

Since she had him standing, Quinn walked her to the door. "You'll find a way. I'll see you then."

By five that evening, Quinn was sick of wallowing in his own thoughts. He'd spent the day on his sofa—trying not to think about making love on it with Diana. He'd put the car race on TV—after moving the pillow she'd blocked the satellite box with. He'd drifted off to sleep a few times, only to be jarred awake by the ringing of the phone. He knew it couldn't be Diana, because they hadn't gotten around to exchanging phone numbers. Still, he was disgusted with himself for being disgusted when it was his own answering service.

None of the day's calls had been as intense as that one from the E.R. this morning, the one that had upset Diana.

She'd been right. That call had been more serious than the average one. As upsetting as it had been for her, her first instinct had been to find out what Quinn needed. To ask if he was okay.

He'd been an ass to laugh off that kind of rare concern. Except when it came to Diana, concern wasn't rare. She was concerned for everyone she met, and for every dog she met, too. She was concerned for men who'd been dead and buried for fifty years on a ranch.

Quinn jackknifed into a sitting position on the couch, determined to deal with this loss once and for all.

Nothing lasts indefinitely.

An ending is an inevitable part of any relationship.

I did my best.

It didn't matter how many times the loop repeated. He couldn't shake the feeling that this relationship shouldn't have died.

Couldn't she see that he was the kind of man who would put some effort into making a girlfriend feel good out of bed as well as in it? Look at how he'd tried to make her feel better about those fifty-year-old graves. He was capable of showing concern, just as she was.

Actually, his mother had been the one to really make her feel better. Hell, Patch the Second had done a great job. Quinn had given her his best all right: his mother and his dog. That was all he had to give a woman.

Quinn got to his feet, scooped a throw pillow off the floor, and pitched it at the sofa. He needed to clear his head. He didn't know why Brian had needed him to take call, but he called him on the chance that Brian could resume phone duties before seven. He could. Quinn transferred call duty back to him, stomped into his boots, grabbed his helmet and headed for his motorcycle.

The bike had been Jamie's, but Quinn had ridden it for him while he was deployed to Afghanistan. Engines that sat unused for a year got gummed up, so Quinn had agreed to drive Jamie's baby a few times a month, just to keep the engine alive. Jamie had surprised them all by returning home from his deployment with a real baby. Since the motorcycle couldn't hold a baby's car seat, and since Quinn had become accustomed to his twice-monthly motorcycle rides, Quinn had bought the bike from Jamie.

He was glad he had. It was good to hear nothing but an engine, one that was loud enough to drown out his thoughts. Most of them.

What happens if I miss you on a Wednesday?

That had been a baffling question. No other woman had ever asked such a thing.

I could have suggested she send a text. I might have been able to call her back between patients.

Even he knew how weak that sounded.

Diana didn't understand his world. She had no idea what the demands were. She sold real estate. She walked dogs at an animal shelter. If she wanted to see someone, she could drop what she was doing and go.

Quinn could not do that, and no matter what Diana thought, it wasn't because he was a jerk. If he played hooky from his job to see his girlfriend, he'd leave a staff of twenty and at least as many patients all sitting in a building he owned, wondering where the hell he'd gone. Some of those patients wouldn't get their ECGs performed and their arrhythmias caught in time. Surgeries in the hospital wouldn't take place, because anesthesiologists expected Quinn to decide if the patient's heart could withstand the procedure.

It was a lot of responsibility, but he'd asked for it. He carried that weight just fine, but damn it, when he had a

Saturday free, it would have been freakin' de-stressing to hold Diana Connor.

That's a booty call.

Not quite. He didn't want just anyone. It had to be Diana. He'd ruined her for champagne; she'd ruined him for any other woman. Not a fair trade.

Quinn took the next entrance ramp to the Mopac. On the expressway, he drove hard and fast, concentrating on the road, listening to the engine roar good and loud at the maximum speed allowed.

Dig a little deeper.

When he thought of Diana, his first image wasn't of her between the sheets. He saw her in green fringe, saying how beautiful the ballroom was, when he could only see her. He saw her in the kitchen with his mom, watching her make potato salad like she was Michelangelo painting a ceiling.

Quinn exited the highway, stopped at a gas station in the middle of nowhere, then headed back to Austin. It was time to stop denying the truth. With Diana, he wanted the out-of-bed part, too. He wanted the pizza by the fire and the walk on the ranch. He wanted a woman who'd make him chase a shelter dog and laugh with him while he did it.

She found the beauty in everyday simplicities from sweet tea to sparkling wine, but from him, she'd expected more. He hadn't given it. No amount of rationalization was going to make the loss of Diana Connor sit easy, not when he couldn't honestly say he'd done his best.

Quinn pulled into her driveway and silenced his motorcycle.

Chapter Twelve

The sound of laughter drifted from the run-down house next door to the brightly painted blue of Diana's 1940s bungalow. From inside Diana's house, Quinn heard nothing, although he'd progressed from civilized knocking to using the side of his fist on her front door.

Her car was in the driveway. She had to be here. Either she was avoiding him, or she was unable to respond. The likelihood that she was seriously injured was infinitesimal, but he'd seen strange cases come through his brother's E.R.

He pounded again, three rapid thuds, and waited. For all he knew, she'd decided to drink away the pain of their parting. It would be easy to have one too many, to pass out, to be in danger. He could walk around the house and look in the windows. If she didn't want to speak to him, that made him something of a trespasser, but if she were alone and incapacitated, he could be a lifesaver.

He raised his fist to knock again—last time, and then he was going to look in her windows—when the door opened and Stewy, sullen Stewy from the shelter, stood there, looking as surprised as Quinn felt.

"Dude, you need to chill. We moved the TV next door."

The kid closed the door in Quinn's face, since Quinn had no response whatsoever.

Okay, he had to give the kid that one. Point to Stewy.

Quinn rubbed a hand over his face, feeling the full scratch of the day's beard, as he readjusted his mental image of what Diana might be doing. He heard a screen door slam in the back of the house and watched Stewy saunter from Diana's backyard to the rear of the shabbier house.

Well, hell. Quinn walked from her neat yard through a stretch of weeds to stand on the edge of what had once been a gravel horseshoe-tossing pit. In the twilight, he watched the group gathered on the large screened-in porch.

His eye went immediately to Diana. This morning's cherry-spangled shirt had given way to a white T-shirt that had stars and hearts sprinkled across her chest, eye-catching shapes made of pink and blue sequins. She was clicking little switches on battery-operated fake candles, setting them into paper lanterns and placing them around the porch. A cluster of six or seven people sat on plastic chairs around a flat-screen television, its picture outshining the lanterns, almost painfully bright to his eyes.

Everyone laughed at something on the screen, and Diana turned to look. Her beautiful, brilliant smile lit everything inside of Quinn. He'd wanted to see her smile; he was annoyed at her smile. Not since a kiss over scrambled eggs had he felt like doing anything close to smiling. How foolish of him to think she'd been missing him the way he'd been missing her.

She seemed to be the hostess of this little party. Done decorating for the coming dark, she traded out some empty bottles for two people, even taking the foam wrap off the empty bottle and putting it on the fresh beer for one guy. Her laughter carried lightly over the others'.

Quinn's mood darkened further. He'd drag the entire party down by walking up. He wouldn't interrupt, then. He'd only come here because Diana had been so upset this morning. His mistake.

Quinn took a step back, gravel crunching under his boot. It looked like partying with the likes of Stewy was all Diana needed to enjoy life.

That's how it looks, but...

Except for the more heavily sequined shirt, Diana looked just as she had yesterday at his mother's picnic, cheerful and attentive to everyone, showing no sign that she'd been unhappy at the graves. Only Quinn had known she was hiding any sadness.

This morning, she'd been unhappy. A woman who left in wet clothes was distressed. None of these people on the porch knew she'd been that upset. None of them ever would, because Diana made it impossible to see anything but her smile.

Quinn stepped forward. He opened the screen door and walked onto the porch just as Stewy came through the house.

"That's a sweet bike out there, Di. Can I use it instead of your car to get the chips?"

"No." Quinn's answer was immediate.

Everyone turned to look at him except Diana. Two

people turned back to the television immediately, uninterested in the latest arrival to the party. One guy lifted his chin in a cool greeting, as if they knew each other. They did not.

"Sorry, Stewy," Diana said, "but the bike isn't mine to give. The keys are in my car."

Without thanking her or acknowledging Quinn, Stewy went back into the house, slamming the front door seconds later.

Quinn saw the slight lift of Diana's chest as she inhaled deeply before she turned to smile at him as if it cost her no effort at all.

"Hello, Quinn. Did you come here on a motorcycle?"

What a silly question.

Diana could not ask all the others that crowded in her head. In her heart.

Why did you come?

Did you miss me?

Are you angry at me?

Why did you come, why did you come, oh, why did you come?

She smiled brightly. "Come and meet my friends." Her introductions were brief, although when she introduced Stewy's single mom and her new boyfriend, who was the only man who stood and shook hands with Quinn, she couldn't help but boast a little. She fussed with the beer bottles in their tub of ice and whispered to Quinn, "I introduced them a few months ago. They're a good match."

Quinn's grin lifted only one corner of his mouth, but it softened the intensity in his expression, and Diana found it easier to breathe.

"Of course," he said.

Why did you come?

They were being so polite. This was nothing like their last, testy talk in his condo. Nothing like their easy walk on the ranch. Nothing like their whispers in the dark.

"So, um, we're all fans of this reality show, so I thought it would be fun to get together to watch it. If you don't know it, I can catch you up on who's who in a jiffy."

Quinn barely glanced at the TV they'd hauled from her house to this one. "No, thanks. I didn't intend to crash a party. Whose house am I barging in on?"

"It's mine." At his raised eyebrow, she explained, "I rent them both, at least for a month or two. I'm going to buy one of them."

"Which one?"

So polite. So interested, hands behind his back, navy T-shirt stretched across his chest.

Diana resolutely kept her eyes on his face, but the gorgeous green of his eyes was hardly less distracting.

"This one, I guess. I painted the other one, but then it looked so cute, the owner decided to raise the price. This one came up for rent, so I grabbed it. These bungalows are in demand. You have to move as soon as they do."

The little crowd around the TV made a united noise of outrage at the antics of one of the show's contestants.

"Do you want to show me the house?" Quinn asked.

Diana knew what he really meant. *Let's go somewhere private to talk.* He had something to say to her, and she had a feeling she wasn't ready to hear it. Then again, another ten minutes of small talk would hardly make her feel prepared, either.

"The kitchen still has a pink stove from the 1950s, and it works. Come and see."

Quinn took his time once they were inside. He actually looked at her house. She'd knocked down most of the cobwebs, thankfully. Still, her industrial broom was propped in a corner, standing guard over all the debris she'd swept out of the way so she could use the back porch tonight.

"You're renting this? I hope it wasn't priced as move-in ready."

"There wasn't a lot of room to negotiate. It is a little discouraging, especially after getting the other one up to speed, but I'm looking at the bright side. The back porch is a definite bonus in a house this size, and the kitchen could really turn out great."

The two of them stopped in the center of the tiny kitchen space. She watched Quinn's fingertips slide over the vintage pink stove. He shook his head at the rounded bubble of the chrome-and-white fridge that was from the same era. Diana thought it was darling, retro and cool, all in one.

With her back against the sink, she had nothing to do but watch Quinn and hold her breath. Her friends had glanced into the kitchen and seen a lot of work. It was crazy, how much she wanted Quinn to see through the surface to the potential underneath.

Quinn put his hands on his hips, filling the girly space with his masculine presence. "It's so you," he said, and then he was smiling and shaking his head and chuckling all at once. "It will be a huge project, but it's so you."

"I think so, too," she said, and she couldn't help but smile back. Suddenly, it was Saturday night all over again, pizza by the fireplace and the right to enjoy his words, his approval, his body. Without further thought, Diana was in his arms and they were kissing, his mouth both exciting and familiar.

They could only take things so far. Laughter erupted on the porch, reminding them they weren't alone.

Quinn took a step with her in his arms, turning her so the fridge was humming at her back when he let her go. He didn't go far, though, and kept his arms braced on either side of her. She looked up at him, and the expression on his face was so much better. Relaxed. Open. Happy.

I'm good for him.

That couldn't be right. They had chemistry, but they weren't a match, not for the long run.

She shouldn't have kissed him again. She shouldn't have let herself have another moment of pretending she belonged to him, of believing they had all the time in the world, when really, their time was up. She'd stolen a weekend with a man who wasn't meant for her, and now she had to pay for that theft.

"I'm sorry," he said, pressing a kiss to her temple.

"For what?" She didn't want Quinn to be mad at himself.

"For this morning. I offended you so badly, you ran away in wet clothes. That's for what."

"It's okay. You were trying to be nice." For both their sakes, she had to let him go. He needed to find his woman in the white gown or the red or blue, the woman who would slide seamlessly into his life, not drive him crazy the way she would.

"It's not okay. I know you like to look on the bright side of everything, but there was nothing positive about the way we ended things this morning."

He bent to kiss the other side of her face, but she

ducked under his arm and retreated back to the sink. He watched her with narrowed eyes.

She cleared her throat. "You're so right. There was nothing positive about it. I'm the one who messed up the ending. It was nice of you to come here, so we could end things on better terms. Now we'll have no hard feelings."

Two hundred pounds of physically fit man was a little scary when it went as still, as deathly still, as Quinn did. Diana didn't mess with large animals that went on alert like that. Not police canines, and not this Mac-Dowell man.

The tension lasted forever, until Diana tried to walk out of the kitchen. Quinn stopped her with a hand on her upper arm. "I didn't come here for a second good-bye. You know that, Diana. *You know that.*"

"I didn't explain it very well this morning, but this is how it should be. We really aren't a good match, Quinn. You aren't the kind of man who can give me what I need."

Quinn turned away from her in the small space. He drove his hand through his hair, making all the muscles across his shoulders move and flex under the tight shirt. "Don't tempt me like that."

"L-Like what?" Diana's heart was pounding, differently than it had been during the kiss, and it seemed like a matter of self-preservation to keep her eyes on this angry, cornered male, to track his every move.

He turned back almost violently. "Don't tempt me to show you what a lot of bull that is. I'm the man who knows exactly what you need."

"I don't mean in bed," she cut him off, feeling something close to anger herself. He wanted her now, but soon enough, he'd be wishing for a woman more like him, and

Diana would become the unwanted pet, the one that was the wrong temperament, the one that was so awkward and painful to place elsewhere. "You're talking about sex. I'm talking about more."

She pushed his chest with both hands and escaped into the living room. It seemed huge, with room to breathe after the confines of that pink-and-white kitchen.

She needed that room to breathe. She never said things in anger like this. When she couldn't keep things positive, she left. Walking away took courage. It was the right way to live. She was proud of going through life avoiding ugly, angry words.

"Tell me." Quinn was right behind her.

She whirled to face him. She took a few steps back, but she couldn't really walk away.

"You were talking about *more*," he said. "I'm listening."

Diana had no words. Nothing, for a man she shouldn't have met, shouldn't have stayed with, shouldn't be so desperate to be with still.

Oh, God. If he didn't let her go, she'd end up like those dogs in the animal shelter, the ones who stood so loyally by their owners' sides while the humans they loved signed the papers to get rid of them. It was heartbreaking. It was what drove her to make good matches, every weekend, for every dog. Yet here she was, so tempted by the wrong man as he walked toward her.

"Tell me, Diana. What's wrong with me?"

"You say you love dogs, but you don't own one."

Quinn stopped short and threw his hands up, a bittersweet reminder of how his mother had reacted when she'd thought her sons were being immature. "What does that have to do with—"

She held her hand up to stop him. She was on the right track; she knew it.

"You don't have a dog, Quinn. Isn't that strange, when you've had them your whole life? You say you love dogs, but you don't. Dogs are demanding, and always present. You don't want a dog, because you wouldn't be able to keep him out of certain areas of your life. The real reason you don't own a dog is because you don't love them enough to tolerate the inconvenience. When you have a hard day, you can't tell a dog you'll let him put his head in your lap and comfort you next Wednesday.

"I'm not saying you are a bad person. I give you credit for knowing your limits. You appreciate dogs. And you would appreciate me as a girlfriend. But I don't want to be appreciated. I want to be loved when I'm underfoot. I want to be loved when it's inconvenient. I do. I want to be loved."

Chapter Thirteen

I want to be loved.

Silence followed her words.

Oh, there was the sound of the ice rattling on the porch as someone helped himself to a fresh beer, the sound of a too-loud commercial break on TV. But between Quinn and Diana, the silence was profound.

I want to be loved.

Was that what she'd been really thinking at the gala, when she'd wondered what would happen if she stopped being the life of the party? If she were the one sitting alone in the corner, wearing black, failing to reflect the light and enjoy the moment?

No one would want that somber version of Diana. No one would come to cheer her up. She knew that; she'd had to contact every person who sat on her porch right now. As long as she made them happy, they'd be her friends.

She'd never in her life intended to find out—ever, with anyone—what would happen if she stopped being positive. But she'd stopped being positive with Quinn just now. In a big way.

She put her hand to her tripping heart. "I can't believe I just said that. Any of that. I'm sorry for being so angry, for—"

"Don't apologize."

She looked up at that.

"You expressed your opinion. It's not the end of the world." He was watching her closely. "You're as white as a ghost. Is there anywhere to sit?"

She did feel kind of strange. She gestured toward the porch, where she'd carried all her patio chairs earlier today, when she'd thought she'd die of the loneliness after leaving Quinn. *Party at my place.* No one had asked her why.

"Let's go out front," Quinn said.

When she didn't move, Quinn took her hand, led her out her own front door, and gently pushed her shoulder to make her sit on the step.

She hadn't called Quinn. He'd come on his own, riding up on a motorcycle to find her tonight. Just her. Not her big-screen TV, not her chips and drinks, just her. She hadn't been positive, or friendly, or happy just now, yet Quinn was still here.

"Why did you come?" she asked. It was easier to talk in the dark.

"I came for this," he said, finding room for himself on the step next to her.

She thought he was going to kiss her. He didn't. He just sat there, staring into the night by her side.

"For what?" she asked.

"To be with you. To hear what you were thinking."

"I wasn't thinking anything nice, apparently." She wrapped her arms around her middle.

"Actually, you were thinking what I was thinking. You just put it in different terms. My relationships have been pretty surface level. I didn't realize how shallow, until today."

He didn't say anything else. He didn't seem to expect her to say anything, either. She had no frame of reference for being with a man, with just one person, for no reason except to sit in the dark. Shouldn't she be *doing* something?

She knew her mother's advice by heart; she had every line of her last letter memorized, the letter she'd written when she was dying, to try to guide Diana through life. There was nothing in it to cover this situation.

Diana was on her own, kicked out of the nest, apron strings cut.

"I missed you, Diana. Seven hours seemed more like seven days."

"Seven months."

She felt him go still again, beside her in the dark, before he spoke. "Then let's keep seeing each other."

"I don't know where it will go," she said. "I've never had a friend like you."

He chuckled, a gentle movement of his chest. "That about sums it up for both of us."

She sighed, and dropped her head on Quinn's shoulder. The muscle was solid. Not relaxed in sleep, not flexed in passion, just solid. There for her.

"When I sigh like you just did," he said, "I know it's time for a ride to clear my head. I brought an extra helmet. Would you like to go nowhere, fast?"

She smiled, although he couldn't see it, turned her head and dropped a kiss on his shoulder.

"I'd love to."

Work should have felt good. It was everything Quinn's personal life had not been for the past two weeks: predictable, defined, controlled. He made his rounds at the hospital, listened to hearts beat, read lab results, deciphered the ECGs he'd ordered. The cardiovascular system embodied physics at its finest, a study of electricity and flow dynamics. Quinn usually found great satisfaction in fixing obstructions and restoring order in the heart and blood vessels of his patients. Usually.

Today, as he drove his truck from the hospital to his office, he was impatient. There'd been more patients in the hospital than usual, so he'd left late, and the streets of Austin were now clogged with rush-hour traffic, doubling his commute to his office. He'd begin seeing his office patients late, which meant he'd be ending his day late, which meant he'd have less of a chance to catch Diana.

Catching her was the operative term. Dating Diana was an experiment in chaos. Her actual work hours were as likely to be from five to nine as nine to five. Even then, she was as likely to be working from a laptop in a burger place as at her desk in her real estate office. Before work, or after, or during, she might disappear to take a rescued mutt to a vet or run some other errand that had been asked of her. She was generous to a fault when it came to doing favors for others.

But when Quinn could catch her...

Yeah.

Quinn caught himself grinning as he entered the

building through the back entrance, smiling even though he was arriving late. He'd smiled more in the past two weeks than he had in the year before he'd met Diana at the gala. The unpredictability of their relationship bothered him, but it also kept him living an absurdly hopeful life. Maybe today they'd grab tacos and watch the bats fly out of the Congress Avenue bridge. Maybe today she'd wear her green dress to dinner at a restaurant with white tablecloths. Maybe today they'd take one look at each other and head straight for his bedroom—or hers. Her bedroom in her blue house, or maybe in the new house, which was the older one.

The woman didn't even have a set address. It drove Quinn crazy. He'd never had to work so hard to find whichever woman he was currently dating.

He greeted members of his staff as he headed down the hallway toward his office, accepting their good-natured teasing.

"Dr. MacDowell in the house. Watch out, he's got his swagger on."

Quinn remembered the first hour he'd known Diana. *I'm here to help you get your party on.* He nearly laughed at the memory.

"Someone's in a good mood…"

One time, Diana had surprised him at his desk after showing a house nearby. Only once in the two weeks they'd been dating, but it was enough to make him hope, every time he opened the door to his inner sanctum, that a woman would be waiting in his office.

"Good morning, darling. You're running late."

Wrong woman. Quinn tried to keep his disappointment from showing. "Morning, Tricia."

Patricia had made herself at home behind his desk,

sitting there as if she owned it. Diana had perched on the edge for only a moment. Like a firefly, she'd flitted from there to the sofa, until she'd perched on the arm of his desk chair. He'd caught her and kept her there for as long as he could.

He picked up the day's mail, which was stacked neatly with its envelopes already sliced open for his convenience. Patricia didn't move from his chair.

"I offered you your own desk once," he reminded her.

"As your office manager?" She made a dismissive motion with one hand. "Please. I don't do hard labor."

"I offered, you said no, so now you don't get my desk."

She moved to the sofa. "Congratulations on your impending uncle-hood. I heard the news at the hospital this morning. You might have told me yourself."

"I didn't know Lana and Braden were making it public yet."

"You wound me. I'm not the public." Patricia crossed her legs. If Quinn didn't know better, he'd think she'd done it just so he'd notice her shapely legs. He doubted any man failed to notice a nice pair of long legs on any woman, but she was Tricia. She didn't need to show off for him. It must be a habit for her to sit just so.

"I heard that your little real estate girl had been there to hear the news, too."

Quinn kept flipping through the mail. "Don't tell me my brothers are turning into gossiping old biddies now that they're married."

"Kendry told me. She's an open book."

"Hardly a challenge for you, then." Quinn led with the opening jab, if only to set a more normal tone for this conversation. Patricia was in an odd mood, and Quinn was running late. Done with his mail, he stood.

Patricia remained seated. She adjusted her watch so that it was facing just the way she wanted it. "Kendry said it was so exciting, toasting Lana's baby and meeting Quinn's girlfriend. Girlfriend? Isn't that a bit much for a fling that didn't last through Sunday brunch?"

"Fishing again. Yes, I'm still seeing her, and she has a name. Diana Connor. Was there any other reason you came by? I'm getting a late start."

"I know her name, darling. My charming step-what-ever sang her praises *ad nauseam* after the gala. Thank God dear Becky's mother retrieved her the next day."

Quinn smiled—inwardly, to himself—at the power of Diana's safety pins, and her kindness.

Patricia extended her hand toward him, wanting a boost up from the plush sofa. Quinn obliged.

She took his white lab coat off its hanger on the back of his door and held it up for him. "The business portion of this visit is a Texas Rescue and Relief service announcement. We've got a meeting this weekend. It's supposed to be a busy hurricane season, and the new director is as nervous as a cat about it. I'm here to drag you to it, if I must."

"I'd forgotten." Quinn slipped his arms in the sleeves.

Patricia smoothed his collar. "No, you didn't. You were hoping I'd forget to force you to come. The fore-casters might be right for once. They upgraded that tropical depression in the gulf to a named storm this morning. I can't tell if dear Karen is hopeful or worried. Anyway, since this will be only the members of the steering committee, I thought we'd hold it at my father's lake house. We can make a boating weekend out of it, if the weather holds."

"That, I definitely can't do." He had a hard enough time catching Diana during the work week. He wasn't about to sacrifice an entire weekend to Patricia and her sailboat fetish.

"Don't be that way. Everyone already agreed to it, and they're bringing their significant others. It will be fun."

The Cargill lake house was a modern-day palace on a massive freshwater lake. If Quinn could corral Diana into coming, he'd have her to himself during the long drive. Once there, she'd be all his, no dogs or people demanding her time and attention.

"In that case, count me in. I'll bring Diana."

"Are you sure? She's not exactly part of our crowd. You might want to leave your little fling at home for this kind of event."

"Let's get two things straight. First, Diana Connor is not a fling. Secondly, you're wrong about her. Take Kendry's word for it, if you don't trust mine. Diana fits in everywhere she goes. You'll like her, I promise."

"Fine. Ten o'clock sharp, then. We have to get the business out of the way so we can relax the rest of the weekend."

"Ten o'clock." Quinn gave her a peck on the cheek. "Now go harass your next victim."

Chapter Fourteen

"**I**'m running late."

"Late is not an option, Diana."

There was no answer on the other end of the line.

Damn it. Too late, Quinn realized the tone of voice he'd used. Diana wasn't a cath lab nurse who'd failed to hand him the proper instrument.

He tried again. "The committee meets at ten. You can't keep other people waiting for no good reason."

More silence. She wasn't an intern who needed a lecture on how the business world worked, either. But damn it, there was a meeting at ten.

The chaos that had marked the first two weeks of their relationship had only worsened since Patricia's invitation. Quinn hadn't seen Diana at all in forty-eight hours. Apparently, it was harder for a part-time animal shelter volunteer like herself to clear her calendar for the weekend than it was for a cardiologist who owned a private practice and served on staff at a major hospital.

He winced at his own thought.

Harder for a shelter volunteer than a cardiologist who needs to check his ego.

Had he always been this unbearably focused on his own life, and was only realizing it since he'd started caring how Diana perceived him?

She suddenly broke the silence, in a stunningly businesslike tone of voice. "I've got a plan. I checked my GPS, and the last errand I have to run is on the way. I'm already in my car, and so is my luggage. If you can be outside your building with your luggage in six minutes, I'll pick you up. We'll run my errand on our way out of town, and we should just make it to the lake by ten."

Quinn never knew what to expect from her, but in this case, the real estate agent who was capable of negotiating a home sale was exactly the version of Diana he needed.

The only problem with her plan, he thought, as he left the cool of his building for the ovenlike heat of June, was that he'd travel to the lake in the passenger seat of a tiny VW Bug. The car was already parked under his building's awning. He heard the trunk latch release as he walked up with his single piece of luggage.

The trunk was already full. A gigantic bag of dog food had been wedged inside. What little room that was left was taken up by a large suitcase in a jarringly bright print of cartoon monkeys. Surely, Diana wasn't making him late for a steering committee meeting of Texas Rescue and Relief because she needed to deliver some dog food. Surely.

She hopped out of the car and came up to him, wearing shorts and a tank top. Plastic gems were sewn around the neckline in a geometric pattern, and her flat thong sandals were made of gold glitter. Quinn was wearing slacks and a dress shirt. Granted, he'd skipped the tie and cuffed his sleeves, but it hadn't occurred to him to let Diana know Patricia's idea of a casual weekend meant the men didn't wear jackets to dinner. When he'd assured Patricia that Diana would fit in...

He scowled at the overcrowded trunk.

"Don't worry," Diana said, "we'll make it all fit."

She sounded cheerful. All morning, every phone call, he'd been on her case, lecturing her about promptness and meetings, and yet, she was smiling at him. She really was the most remarkably happy person he'd ever been around.

"You look beautiful." He let go of his luggage handle—what an idiot to be holding luggage when he could be holding this woman—and crowded her against the open trunk as he took her mouth the way she always seemed to inspire him to: fully. Completely. Passionately.

All weekend. He'd have her in arm's reach all weekend, and he'd have her in some undoubtedly plush bed all night. He could feel his heart beat harder. Hell, he could practically hear the blood rushing past his ears as it left his brain and headed south. He could hear...

He could hear...

The deep bass of a dog barking. A large dog. One that sounded like it might consume a gigantic bag of dog food.

He stopped kissing her. "You don't have a dog with you."

She couldn't be so...so...*clueless*. As soon as he thought it, he felt a distinct pain in his chest, a physical sensation that might have been the first crack in his confidence in them as a couple.

She kept smiling, oblivious. "There had to be a reason I had dog food in here, right?"

"Your car isn't big enough to carry the dog food and your luggage and my luggage and me *and the dog.*"

She waved away his pronouncement on her car's capacity and glanced from the trunk to the tiny excuse for a backseat. "I've got it. Let's put the dog food in the backseat and the dog on top of it, like it's his bed. Then you get the front seat, and the luggage gets the trunk."

He would not acknowledge the crack. He refused to feel the pain. He could function without feeling emotions. It was a vital skill for a doctor who threaded wires into human hearts.

He hauled the dog food out of the trunk while she opened the passenger-side door and hauled the dog out of the car. It was a damned Saint Bernard, or at least mostly that breed. In a Bug. She kept the dog out of traffic with two hands on its collar while Quinn laid the heavy bag on the seat.

Quinn started to put his single, compact, efficient carry-on piece into the trunk next to her large monkey-print bag.

"Wait a second," Diana called out. With one hand on the dog, she hauled a second piece of luggage off the front seat, this one covered in a banana design. Of course. "Can you put this in the trunk?"

"Barely."

The dog was eager to get back in the car and away from the noise of the traffic. It quickly became clear that he was not going to fit on top of the dog food in the backseat. Quinn took both pieces of her luggage out of the trunk, making a splash of color on the gray asphalt.

Like putting together pieces of a two-layered puzzle, Quinn squeezed his bag and her larger one into the trunk with the dog food and slammed it shut. His dress shirt was sticking to his back in the hundred-degree Texas heat.

"See?" she said. "It fit."

"That dog and your smaller bag will both need to fit into the backseat."

In the end, they did, but only when Quinn brought his seat so far forward that he literally had to hug his knees. "Let's just get going. Please."

Diana began chatting. Quinn had seen her do it before, when she was trying to cover up an unhappy feeling. Well, he felt unhappy, too, so he sank into silence while she gabbed away.

"I'm sorry about the dog food. I made him some scrambled eggs this morning, since I was out. I usually have some in the house, but I didn't know he was coming for a visit. His owner needed someone to care for him for an extra day."

Naturally, she'd made herself available to the unknown owner. Quinn came last in her list of priorities. He was torn between feeling sorry for himself and being worried for her. She claimed to be happy when she felt needed and helpful, but Quinn thought she was being more of a doormat than she knew.

Quinn said nothing, and Diana's chatter resumed.

"We're on our way," she said, a chipper little skipper of the lime-green Bug. "I didn't have the car last night to get to the store for more dog food, so it was lucky I had a pot roast in the freezer. He loved it."

Whether two-legged or four-legged, what male wouldn't love to have Diana fawning all over him, dropping everything to make him a pot roast?

She could have called him. He could have brought her a bag of dog food. Diana shut him out of her world. Except for the volunteers at the shelter and the TV-watching crew he'd met so briefly that first weekend, Diana kept him carefully separate from her friends. From her real life.

We really aren't a good match, Quinn. She'd said it so earnestly, standing in front of her retro refrigerator.

It bothered him. If she continued to shut him out of her life, then her prediction would certainly come true.

Quinn was going to set a different tone this weekend by fully including her in his life. His friends were going to love her. Diana needed to see that her fears about being a poor match for him outside the bedroom were unfounded.

He supposed breaking his silence would be a good step toward his weekend goals.

"Why didn't you have your car last night?" he asked.

"I had to loan it to someone."

His friends wouldn't mooch off her. They'd never borrow her car. They kept their dogs at canine spa facilities.

Diana began turning down side streets. The dog's owner lived near the highway, all right. Close enough to make the property undesirable, judging by the neighborhood.

"Leave the air running, I'll be right back," Diana said. She was out of the car and coaxing the dog to squeeze out in a flash. Quinn watched through the windshield as she wrestled the animal to the door of the shabby duplex.

Then she returned to the trunk and started unpacking the suitcases to get to the dog food.

The owner of the Saint Bernard was apparently content to let Diana not only buy the dog food but to haul it up the cracked sidewalk herself. Cursing inwardly, Quinn released his shoulder belt and got out of the car.

Without a word, Quinn reached into the trunk to sling the fifty-pound bag over his shoulder and followed Diana to the duplex. An unkempt man stood in the door, watching them sweat as they approached. The man couldn't stir himself to meet them halfway, apparently. Couldn't help the woman who'd watched his dog on short notice. Diana smiled and chatted and accepted his rudeness in a way that made Quinn feel close to boiling over.

He dropped the bag at the doorstep.

"What's this?" the guy mumbled around the cigarette dangling from his lower lip.

"How about 'thank you'?" Quinn challenged him.

"I don't take charity."

"Good, then you can pay Diana for this bag of dog food."

Diana looked alarmed. "Don't be silly. The dog food just goes with the dog."

The man glared at her, looking as surly as Stewy on steroids. "You keep it."

"I don't have a dog. What would I do with dog food?" She giggled and nodded as if she were making perfect sense. It was an act, of course, and Quinn could see it was an act, but Diana apparently knew what she was doing. When she said, "We'll just move the bag inside," the guy shrugged instead of keeping up his argument.

Quinn didn't like the guy's lack of gratitude. *Move it*

inside your damned self, he started to say, but stopped when he saw the man was balancing on one leg. His only leg.

Quinn felt like an ass. He hauled the bag over the threshold, then turned toward the man in silent question. When the man jerked his chin toward the kitchen, Quinn obeyed and set the bag against the wall by the battered refrigerator.

The man was uncomfortable with the help. He'd already stated he wasn't a charity case, but he couldn't have much money. Diana had clearly been trying to save his pride by insisting she had no use for the dog food, so he might as well take it.

Diana said her goodbyes to the mammoth St. Bernard. She offered her hand to the amputee in a businesslike manner, another subtle way to make the man feel they were equals, not charity-giver and helpless recipient. While the man shook her hand, Quinn saw him set his other on the waist-high dog's head for balance.

Diana had made another brilliant match.

She wasn't making Quinn late by running a frivolous errand. She hadn't let herself be taken advantage of, either, but had instead deliberately spent her money on someone she deemed a worthy cause. Most of all, she wasn't clueless, and Quinn was ashamed of himself for having thought it. So how did a man go about apologizing without explaining what he'd thought?

Diana was silent as they drove out the other side of the duplex's semicircular drive. Quinn slid his seat back as far as it would go, then angled himself to watch her as she drove. She was beautiful, flushed from the heat, but she was blinking a little too rapidly. He hoped they were tears of pride in herself.

"Do you remember the morning after our one-night stand?" he asked.

She kept her eyes on the road, but wrinkled her nose at his question.

He persisted. "I said that I knew I was lucky to be with you, do you remember that?"

"Yes." She waited at the red light that would let them onto the highway's entrance ramp.

"I was right that morning, but every day, I find out that I was more right than I knew. That was a beautiful thing you did, finding a way to help that man when he was dead set against receiving help. Your instincts about people amaze me."

"Aw, shucks," she said, trying to be humorous when he could see he'd made her blush with his praise.

His silence was well-intentioned this time. She needed a minute to soak in a compliment without laughing it off.

"I hardly know what to say to that," she said.

"For me, it was a lesson in humility. I'll never doubt your errands are important, and your matchmaking skills are phenomenal."

Then, because he was making her tear up when she needed to be clear-eyed to drive, and because Diana preferred laughter, always, he tried for a little humor. "If all that weren't humiliating enough, I also have to deal with the fact that I now know I got kicked out of your bed last night to make room for a Saint Bernard."

Her laughter warmed his heart, but that crack of doubt wouldn't go away completely. A few carefree miles passed before he put together the details.

Diana was a phenomenal matchmaker, a woman who understood others instinctively.

We really aren't a good match, Quinn.

The icy feeling returned to his chest.

Chapter Fifteen

The gas gauge was dangerously—and unsurprisingly—near empty. Diana had hoped to make it to the lake without having to run that errand. It was nearly ten when she pulled into the gas station.

"I'll be super quick."

She could have saved her breath. Quinn was already out of the car, sliding his credit card into the pump with one hand and removing her car's gas cap with the other. He didn't seem angry, just focused. Very doctor-ly. This made sense, since she was making him late to a doctor-ly meeting.

Anger, though, might have been more normal. It wasn't that she didn't appreciate his restraint, and all his kind words about how important her errands had been. After all, spending the past hour's drive to the lake in a tiny car with an angry bear wouldn't have been too pleasant for her, but she was the reason he was late to an important meeting, and she knew it.

Despite Quinn's apparent good mood, Diana was getting nervous. It didn't have much to do with making a meeting on time. It had more to do with entering a foreign world, one where everyone would focus on hard things. Natural disasters. Human suffering. How was a person supposed to look on the bright side of such things?

She couldn't, and she was afraid to spend a weekend with a group of people who were tough enough to actually seek out tragic situations.

It's just a party on a lake. It will be fun.

She ought to be more excited. Last summer, she'd had a ball at a friend's house on this same lake. They'd drunk sweet wine coolers and eaten salty potato chips on his dock. He'd owned a Jet Ski, and Diana had taken a turn on it. Maybe Patricia would have a Jet Ski, and Diana could ride behind Quinn, the way she did on his motorcycle. That would make for a fun weekend.

First, however, there would be some kind of business meeting. Quinn was wearing work clothes. No tie and stethoscope, but still, slacks and a button-down shirt didn't exactly scream "lake house weekend" to her. She wasn't part of the meeting, but Patricia would be. Patricia wasn't afraid of natural disasters.

Diana bet Patricia wouldn't be in shorts and a tank top, either.

It was too late to pack a different wardrobe, but Diana had brought a long-sleeved white shirt to wear over her bikini. If she wore it over her tank top now, she'd arrive looking a little less casual. She popped the trunk and went to find—

Nothing. Her banana suitcase was gone. She quickly checked the backseat, but only her monkey luggage was there, the one containing her makeup and hair dryer, and the bottle of champagne she'd bought for a hostess gift. Her bathing suit was in there. Nothing else to wear.

She'd taken the luggage out to get to the dog food. It was probably sitting in the duplex's semicircular driveway. Or, more likely, it had been stolen by now.

She shut the trunk, maybe with a little more force than she'd intended to.

"What's wrong?" Quinn asked, watching her as he pumped the gas.

There's enough misery in the world without me adding mine to it. Diana forced a smile. She'd already made him haul dog food in dress clothes. She'd already made him late to his meeting. She wasn't going to complain about something neither he nor she could fix.

"I hope you really, really like my outfit. It's the only one I've got with me."

The awkwardness began in earnest when they reached the iron gates. Diana rolled her window down, but before she could push the call button on the security box, a man's voice came through the speaker.

"Your name, please."

"Diana Connor."

There was a brief pause. "Are you expected?"

Quinn leaned across her. "Quinn MacDowell."

He had that tone to his voice again, the one that said he was in charge, so listen up.

The security guard did. "Good morning, Dr. Mac-Dowell. Welcome back." The gates began swinging open.

Of course. Diana Connor meant less than nothing in a place like this. She drove her little Bug several hundred yards to the edge of a cliff. Miles of blue-green water were visible beyond a modern house.

She pulled into a large parking area to the left of the house. Diana popped the trunk, but when they got out of the car, Quinn casually shut it again with one hand and took her keys. "Don't worry, they'll get the luggage."

Awkward, but interesting. Diana wondered who "they" were. The two-story house was elegant and expensive-looking with its natural stone exterior, but it didn't look big enough to hold all the people that must have arrived in the other cars. The entire bottom floor was a four-car garage. From the parking area, curving stone stairs were set into the hillside that sloped up to the top story's rather grand double doors.

As they reached the top of the stairs, one of the doors opened and an older gentleman in khaki slacks and a navy blazer greeted Quinn.

They stepped inside. Diana experienced a fleeting sense of vertigo, for they were standing in a spacious marble foyer at the top of a polished marble staircase. Beyond the iron railing, there was nothing but open space to the floor below. The lake view was spectacular through the two-story-tall windows.

Diana turned back to their host, and stuck her hand out to the gentleman. "You must be Mr. Cargill. Thank you so much for inviting us." She wished she'd thought to pull the champagne out of her monkey suitcase to give him.

The man shook her hand briefly, then let go and tucked both hands behind his back. "You are welcome here, miss, but I am not Mr. Cargill. He is not currently in residence."

Awkward. So very awkward.

Quinn put his hand on the small of her back and handed her car keys to the...whatever he was. The butler? Did people really have butlers?

The sound of a woman's heels coming briskly up the marble stairs was followed immediately by the appearance of Patricia. Well, the top half of Patricia. She stopped once she'd climbed high enough to see them. "You're here. Finally."

Quinn kept his hand on Diana's back as they started down the stairs. Her sandals didn't make an elegant clicking sound with her every step. They were completely flat, so they sounded about as glamorous as bedroom slippers as she walked down to Patricia's stair.

Patricia kissed Quinn on the cheek. Her hair was up in a French twist. Her silk navy blouse topped wonderfully flowy gray slacks, and she looked cool and sophisticated and every inch at home.

Diana felt underdressed and disheveled, like a woman who'd hauled a Saint Bernard in and out of her car all morning in the Texas summer heat.

"You remember Diana Connor from the gala." Quinn's introduction sounded so formal, but it fit the surroundings.

"Of course. The real estate agent. How nice to see you again." Without offering her hand or a peck on the cheek, Patricia turned back to Quinn and took his arm. "You're late, darling."

"Only ten minutes."

"I've held this meeting for as long as I possibly could, but we have so much to cover."

"I think Texas Rescue will manage to operate this year despite a ten-minute delay."

With that dryly delivered line, Diana knew she'd come full circle. The urbane man in a tuxedo was back, the unflappable one, the one who didn't laugh.

Or rather, Diana was back in his world.

She'd invaded this world once, naively thinking it would be a lark to go to a formal gala. She'd stolen a perfect moment by dancing with Quinn, then a perfect night, and a weekend. For three weeks, she'd been stealing moments with a man whom she never should have met. And now, in this lakeside mansion, she'd come back to the world where people wore silk and had butlers.

"Diana, do join us in the meeting room after you've had a chance to…freshen up." Patricia looked toward the top of the stairs. "I see Robert has your luggage. He'll show you to your room."

"This is all I've got," Diana said, tapping the neckline of her shirt. She smiled as she said it, so that Patricia wouldn't feel sorry for her or be concerned that her guest felt embarrassed—although her guest most certainly did. Heck, even if she'd had her luggage, Diana wouldn't have had anything appropriate to change into. Then again, that was the bright side: the forgotten suitcase gave her the perfect excuse for being so underdressed.

Quinn started shepherding them down the stairs. "We had a luggage mishap on the way here."

"Oh?" Patricia said invitingly, and Diana braced herself for a retelling of her dumb move with the dog food.

Awkward. Diana would have to laugh at her own stupidity.

Quinn didn't offer any details, however. "Since my ten-minute delay has already upset your sense of punc-

tuality, let's go straight to the meeting. I assume everyone is in the billiards room?"

Quinn was watching out for her. She knew he was
just as bothered by arriving late as Patricia was, but he
was being a gentleman by not blaming Diana. The same
was true of the way he hadn't said that Diana had left
her luggage on the ground and driven away like an idiot.
Everyone could have had a good chuckle at her absent-
mindedness, but it really wasn't funny, and Diana was
grateful to be spared.

But no matter how kind Quinn was being toward her,
Diana was the odd man out in this house. She stayed by
his side as they walked through the gorgeous great room,
which was furnished with dark, carved woods and rich
leather upholstery, a well-designed interior that could
hold its own against the spectacular lake view. It was
undeniably magnificent, but it was meant to impress,
and Diana felt all the intimidation it dished out.

Patricia walked on Quinn's other side, chatting easily
with him like the friend and colleague she was. Diana
fell back a step, intentionally, when they reached another
staircase to descend to a third level that hadn't been visible from the driveway. From her step behind them, it
was easy to admire Quinn and Patricia. They looked so
elegant together, moving in sync in their well-tailored
clothes against the backdrop of this mansion.

They'd looked just as good together at the gala.

Patricia put her hand on Quinn's arm casually—or
perhaps, not so casually. She cast one smooth glance at
Diana over her shoulder. Diana absorbed all the impact
of that single, well-designed look: she was the guest of
a woman who didn't want her in her home.

Diana couldn't blame her. She was, after all, sleeping with the man who was Patricia's perfect match.

Awkward didn't begin to describe it.

Quinn remained standing with Diana as Karen Weaver opened the meeting with a weather update. There was one chair available, but he was half of a couple. Party of two, and Patricia knew it. Hell, he'd brought Diana at her invitation.

The billiards table had been converted into a conference table courtesy of a custom-made wood top Quinn had always admired. Matching club chairs, handmade to be just the right height, were drawn up to the table. All eight of them. But Diana made nine.

Quinn made a small gesture toward the single empty chair as he skewered Patricia with a look.

"So with these new tracking projections, New Orleans is breathing easier, but the Texas coast is not," Karen said.

Patricia stood and walked over to one of the captain's chairs that sat around the low poker table. Quinn joined her, and picked up a chair to move it closer. It was too short, but there was no other choice. He'd use it.

"Where are everyone else's guests?" he asked Patricia under his breath. The pool deck lay just outside the billiards room, but the only person he could see out there was a staff member setting rolled towels on the vacant chairs.

"Marcel took them out on the sailboat. You just missed them."

Quinn felt no need to hide his displeasure. "You couldn't have waited ten minutes to send them off? Diana's now the odd man out."

"Are you her babysitter or her paramour? Surely she can handle the disappointment of missing a boat ride."

In the split-second before Quinn could set her straight, Patricia, very wisely, backpedaled. "I'll fix it, Quinn. Take the chair."

Karen sounded distressed as she concluded her update. "Four of the five weather service models are projecting landfall on Monday." She paused to look around the table. "And we're understaffed."

Patricia addressed the room. "Then I'm so glad Quinn brought an extra set of hands. Does everyone know Diana Connor?"

With that, Patricia "fixed it" by forcing Diana to participate in the meeting for the next half hour. To Quinn, it was like watching a master class in how to be bitchy without actually saying anything rude. It started with Patricia moving her papers graciously so that Diana could have her chair, keeping her far enough away that Quinn couldn't speak to her on the side. Patricia used the short captain's chair, if standing in front of it counted as using it. That seemed generous of her, but it wasn't. From her standing position, Patricia easily took over the meeting from the seated director. Karen was no match for Patricia.

Diana seemed hopeful that the weekend would be cut short. "If you need the hospital to open on Tuesday, then will you go down now to set up, before the storm hits?"

Patricia answered in a perfectly civil way, but there was something nasty about her explanation that Quinn couldn't put his finger on. "Going down today or tomorrow puts us in the path of the storm. We can't handle casualties if we put ourselves in a position to become casualties. Besides, my volunteers will need to use Monday to arrange their schedules. Doctors cannot just leave their practices with no notice. I do hope your job is not as demanding."

"I hope so, too," Karen said. "I'd love for her to come with us."

Quinn decided he liked the new director, no matter what Patricia's issue with her was.

Diana declined. "I don't think I'd be very good in a crisis."

"Please, join us," Patricia said. "I'm sure we can use your help."

And…bitchy Patricia was back. Quinn could just *tell*. Damn it, he needed to intervene, but how did he intervene against politeness?

Patricia referred to a document in her hand. "We were looking at our areas of personnel shortage earlier this week. What can you do? I need nurses—no. Medical assistant—no. Are you CPR certified? We'd need to have an actual certification on file by Tuesday. No?"

Karen interrupted, looking as uncomfortable as the others around the table. "There is always a need for clerical work."

"Oh, yes," Patricia agreed. "Let's see. Have you any experience as a comptroller? Have you ever worked in a pharmacy? Perhaps you could alphabetize the medicines."

Diana never stopped smiling. She never showed any distress. But Diana, apparently, had had enough.

"Alphabetizing," Patricia repeated. "Shall I put you down for that?"

"That depends," Diana said, "on whether or not you

need my alphabet certification on file by Tuesday. Kindergartens require more notice than one working day to send a transcript."

Chapter Sixteen

"You handled yourself beautifully."

"I offended our host." Diana thought Quinn was a little too proud of her for being less than a gracious guest.

"Your host offended you first. It was perfectly fair to hit back."

The meeting had dragged on for hours, but now the fun was supposed to begin. They'd come to their assigned bedroom to change clothes, so they were talking while Quinn wore surfer's board shorts and she wore an orange bikini. It was a strange way to have a discussion on ethics.

"I was taught to turn the other cheek," she said.

"You did turn it. Patricia wasn't going to stop until you made her. Think of her as the one dog that annoys the rest for no good reason. You made her sit and be quiet for a moment." He leaned against the footboard of the king-size bed and shook his head as he watched her brush her hair. "I can't believe your bathing suit happened to be in the monkey luggage. If it had been lost with the banana bag, we'd have the perfect excuse to skip Patricia's idea of a pool party."

"I'm not going to do anything else to hurt her feelings." In fact, Diana had spent every minute since her smart-alecky exchange trying to prove that she was normally a nice person. She'd run up the stairs and out to Karen's car to fetch some paperwork for her. When the other guests had come back from their sail around the lake, she'd shaken hands cheerfully and even brought a few thirsty guests some drinks.

"You did a great job defending yourself. How should we celebrate?"

Quinn scooped her up and tossed her on their bed, then followed by diving onto the mattress next to her, landing on his stomach like some kind of crazed baseball player sliding headfirst into home base. "We're both horizontal and nearly naked. Got any ideas?"

He was darned adorable when he was playful like that, but the man was so not getting to home base. Not now, at least.

"Everyone is out by the pool," Diana said, giving his shoulder a push, as if she could make a two-hundred-pound man roll off a bed.

"Good. They won't miss us."

"Patricia wants us to enjoy the water before dinner. You guys have a hard week ahead of you." It wasn't in Diana to deliberately offend someone who was trying to make sure others had a good time. If Patricia wanted everyone to enjoy themselves by the pool, then Diana wouldn't, couldn't refuse to go.

Quinn obviously did not feel obliged to be so obliging. He began kissing Diana, skipping her mouth and her neck and her breasts to start with her soft stomach, exposed as it was in her bikini. Her soft, ticklish stomach. Diana began to giggle and push harder at his shoulder.

There was a knock at the bedroom door, followed by Patricia's voice. "Hello? Is it safe to come in?"

"No," Quinn hollered.

The doorknob turned, anyway, and Diana scrambled off the bed.

The door itself only opened a few inches. "I thought since my guest had lost her luggage, she might need a maillot."

Diana wasn't sure what a "My Yo" was, but then a slender hand reached through the crack and dropped a white bunch of material onto the floor.

"See you in a few." The door shut.

Quinn cursed, and he sounded halfway serious.

Diana picked up the white material and held it up to herself. It looked for all the world like a one-piece bathing suit to her, but it was a *maillot*. And it was clearly too big.

"It's a good thing I've got safety pins."

Quinn had rolled to his back and tucked his hands behind his head. "You are not wearing that. Your bathing suit looks great."

At her hesitation, he sat up. "Seriously, your bathing suit looks *great*. Why would you put on one that doesn't fit?"

"When someone tries to do something nice for you," she began carefully, thinking it through as she said it out loud, "the only proper response is 'thank you,' and to accept it."

"That sounds like one of your mottos. Your mother's?" He asked the question while looking at her so intently, she felt defensive for no real reason.

"She left me an etiquette book. It's in there."

Quinn stared at her a minute longer. "Let me tell you what's not in the etiquette book. Some people might give you a gift to manipulate you. And as strange as it may seem to you, some people will like you better if you see right through them and refuse to play along with their demands. Patricia respects you for the way you fielded her certification garbage today."

Diana wondered if Quinn was aware that he knew Patricia so well. Someday, he'd see what was under his nose, and Patricia would effortlessly fit into his life as his lover instead of his friend.

Until then, Patricia was Quinn's friend and Diana's hostess for the weekend, two good reasons for Diana to play nice.

"If you want to do her a favor, then don't fawn all over her." Quinn got off the bed. "Let's hit the pool before you cave in to her machinations. I will definitely be unhappy if you take off that orange bikini. No—that's not true. I'd love to see you take it off. But not at the pool. You know what I mean."

Diana laughed, but a brilliant idea had just hit her. She hadn't given Patricia that ridiculously expensive bottle of champagne yet. She could catch her and present it as a peace offering.

"You go out to the pool. I'll be right there."

Diana didn't want to walk around the house in nothing but a bikini, so she wore Quinn's dress shirt as a cover-up. After pulling the flower-painted bottle from her suitcase, she looked out the bedroom window toward the pool deck, but she didn't see Patricia. She headed up the stairs to the middle level, where the kitchen flowed into the rest of the living space.

Women were talking in the kitchen. Diana hesitated on the stairs. Their voices were not muffled at all, but sounded amplified by the granite countertops and polished stone floors.

"Don't you think it's time for you to seduce Quinn? Please? That girl has got to go."

Diana couldn't identify the speaker by her voice, but she recognized Patricia when she answered.

"If I sleep with him, then I'll be just like you. And Bethany Valrez. And all the others. You played the short game."

"That's the only game there is with him. It's a very enjoyable game, too. I don't know what you're waiting for, but I won't be able to stand having her around for the rest of the year. Do us all a favor and make your move."

Diana sagged against the banister, clutching the champagne to her chest. She was less shocked to hear that everyone expected Patricia to be with Quinn than she was to hear that Quinn had once been lovers with one of the other women. How did they stay so perfectly civilized? For the rest of her life, after she and Quinn broke up, if Diana ran into Quinn anywhere, she would blush ten shades of red and not be able to look him in the eye.

Patricia addressed her kitchen buddies like she was running another planning committee. "I'm in it for the long game. I mean more to him precisely because I haven't slept with him. When the whole game is over, I'll be the last one standing."

"Game over? You think he's ready for marriage?" This, from a third woman.

The first woman followed up. "If you think you can bring him to the altar, more power to you, but would you hurry it up? That house in Catalina will be available in October, and the guys are willing to go. If Quinn brings her, I'll gag."

"She's the last hurrah for his bachelorhood." Patricia sounded confident. "His brothers are married now. That always spooks a man at first, so he's chosen someone totally inappropriate. Someone he'd never settle down with."

Diana bit her lip, adding a little physical pain to the hurtful words. Patricia would be shocked to know that Diana agreed with her. She'd always known she wasn't a good match for Quinn, but hearing Patricia say Quinn wanted her precisely because of that made it worse.

The Catalina woman was still impatient. "I cannot be seen with a girl who wears glitter on her feet and plastic jewels on her boobs."

"I'll be engaged to Quinn within six months, mark my word. But I've got to let him overdose on her first. He won't appreciate it if I chase her away. I'm throwing them together as often as possible, in every situation. He'll be embarrassed by her sooner or later."

"Sooner, if I know you."

"By October, please."

Diana sat on the step. It cut to the bone to hear how very little the other women wanted her around. She'd been so naive, thinking that Patricia was like the high-spirited Dalmatian at the animal shelter, the one who'd pushed to be in charge constantly. That dog had never calculated how to cause the downfall of any human it knew.

Anger set in, pushing the hurt aside. She'd complimented Patricia on the house, the view, the food. She'd thanked Patricia for her hospitality, when she'd been invited only so that Quinn would see her as a misfit.

To know that the other women wanted her to make a fool of herself was infuriating. How friendly had she been to them today? Diana had memorized their names. She'd brought them glasses of water. They'd kept her hopping, no doubt hoping that Quinn would see her as some kind of underling.

She should leave. It would take courage, but it would be the right thing to do, to simply return home. In a situation this negative, what could she possibly gain by staying?

She'd make up some excuse, something to keep Quinn from being embarrassed when his date left the weekend party early. She'd get in her green Bug and drive away.

And leave him behind, with all these nasty people?

It was exactly what they wanted.

For once in her life, Diana didn't want to make people happy.

Screw them.

Those two ugly words felt kind of perfect. Diana gripped her champagne bottle by the neck, stood, and marched up the stairs. She walked into the kitchen, head high, the tails of Quinn's dress shirt fluttering behind her, and started opening cabinet doors, looking for the champagne flutes.

"Can I help you find something?" Patricia asked, in a tone so helpful, it was hard to believe it was a lie.

"Champagne flutes." She held up the bottle. "This is

Quinn's favorite. I thought we'd make ourselves scarce for a little while. You know."

Patricia could have her "turn" some other time in the far, far future. Diana wanted to make it clear that for this weekend, Quinn was hers.

Patricia thought Quinn would hate an overdose of her? Diana almost laughed at the thought. He was going to love every minute.

"Oh, honey. That's not the same thing we were drinking at the gala."

Patricia reached for the bottle. Diana let it go only to avoid a demeaning tug of war.

"Good Lord, it's warm," Patricia said, and Diana saw her make a face of horror at one of her friends. She opened the glass-fronted wine refrigerator and pulled out another champagne bottle. It was also painted with flowers. "Let me help you. These come from the same *maison,* but they are hardly equal."

She set the bottles on the counter, side by side, but had barely started a lecture about champagnes that did or did not have vintage years on their labels, when Quinn came into the kitchen.

Everyone stopped staring at Diana and looked at him.

After a brief, frozen moment, Quinn looked at Diana and started to smile, one slow, sexy smile that took its time spreading over his face. Only then did he walk up to her.

"You are just the woman I wanted to see."

Quinn didn't know precisely what he'd walked into, but Diana looked a little pale and tight-lipped. It had taken him a fraction of a second to put the details together. One, he'd seen her look like that once before, after she'd gotten angry in her pink kitchen. Two, the other women in the kitchen were all angled toward her like a pack of hunting dogs. Three against one.

He was sure there'd been one of those mysterious female showdowns. Quinn didn't like the odds Diana had been facing. He hoped his deliberate smile and the way he stood next to her made it clear that he was on her side.

She looked so damned desirable in his shirt, it took him a moment to notice the two bottles of champagne on the countertop. He recognized the painted flowers. The gala. She'd tried to bring him the champagne from the gala.

He picked up the less expensive bottle, knowing she hadn't spent a thousand dollars on the other one. He had no doubt that Patricia had brought it out to show Diana that her bottle wasn't good enough.

It was more than good enough. It touched him in a way that was so sweet, it was on the verge of painful.

"You brought this for us?" he asked her.

His doubts vanished. He held that bottle in his hand, and tried not to be overwhelmed by its significance. If he'd worried that their relationship wasn't going well, this bottle proved otherwise. A woman didn't plan a private champagne toast with a man she still considered a bad match.

To hell with their audience. To hell with being civilized, with all the snarky comments and smug superiority he'd been so aware of this day. The woman who'd brought him this gift was worth having, and by God, he was going to have her.

He put the bottle down to take her face in both hands, and he whispered a simple thank-you over her lips. For a beautiful, brief moment, with a single slide of tongues that was as close to perfect as a physical act could be, he let himself enjoy the intimate interior of her mouth. He ended the kiss, slowly let his hands leave her face, and picked up the champagne.

"Let's go," he said.

The other women in the kitchen were like statues, all staring at him. He saluted them with the bottle. "Don't hold dinner for us."

As he led Diana outside, he clearly heard a woman's voice reverberate off the granite and stone.

"Do you still think he'll be yours in six months?"

Chapter Seventeen

The beautiful thing about champagne was that a man could open it without a corkscrew. With six efficient turns of his wrist, Quinn knew the wire cage would come off, the cork could be eased out and Diana would be his.

He took the first swig straight from the bottle. It was warm, and the carbonation was sharp. He'd never had anything so delicious in his life.

"What should we drink to first?"

His voice filled the tunnel-like space of the boathouse, bouncing off the cavernous wooden structure in the dark. The late afternoon sun was blindingly bright on the water beyond the garage-style door, but inside, everything was cool and dark. Jet Skis and two-person sailboats bobbed at their moorings as he and Diana stood on the wood dock that ran the length of the space.

Diana started kicking off her gold sandals, looking over her shoulder and into the dark corners of the building. Her whisper blended with the lapping sound of the water. "Are you sure this is private?"

Quinn stepped close to her, one leg brushing the inside of her thigh, and bent to whisper low in her ear. "Very private. Let's drink champagne and make love."

She shivered, a delicate movement that brushed her covered breasts lightly against his bare arm, a simple sensation that sent his body from ready to shockingly hard. He wanted Diana with an intensity that gave every caress urgency. "Hold this," he said, his voice gruff in the echoes as he pressed the champagne bottle into her hand. He pulled his T-shirt off and threw it on top of her discarded sandals. "Drink to us."

She did, tilting her head back and swallowing as he kissed her throat. His hands weren't steady, a tremor betraying his emotion, not the hands of a doctor at all, as he pushed his dress shirt off her shoulders and reached behind her neck to pull the ties of her orange top, skimming down her waist to pull the ties at her hip. The scraps of cloth fell to the floor, and the sight of her before him nearly felled him, too. He pressed her to his body, the sensation of skin on skin as shattering as he'd ever known it, and he staggered back to sink onto the boat cushions that had been stacked against the wooden wall, ready for summer days.

In the darkness of the boathouse, Diana was a vision of pale skin, a work of art, womanly and beautiful as she straddled him. Silently, she passed him the champagne so she could release his body, untying the surfer's shorts that kept him from her, slipping her hand into his pocket to find a foil packet, and then he was once more insanely, intensely grateful when she took him into her.

He would always be grateful for the gift of Diana. He knew it, had known it from the first, but this time, he allowed the truth of it into his heart. He felt it with every roll of their hips, until he had to whisper it into the skin of her chest, her neck, her ear. "I want this forever, Diana. Forever."

How could something that felt so right be so very, very wrong?

Diana rested against Quinn, relaxed, no muscle in her body remaining tense after the release of making love. Her heart beat steadily, slowing while she watched the rhythmic motion of the boats bobbing so slightly with the motion of the water in the boathouse. It was a perfect moment in time.

And yet, she felt like the terrible person she was. For weeks now, since the night she'd met Quinn MacDowell, she'd worried about herself. She'd made memories with a man whom she'd known was not for her, and she'd dreaded her own inevitable heartbreak.

Not once had she worried about Quinn.

Forever, he'd said.

She wouldn't be the only one who got hurt.

Diana stared at the boats for one more minute, imprinting the peacefulness in her mind. Then she sat up. Bent over, retrieved her bikini from the dock. Started tying it on. She felt like a robot. That was good. She didn't want to feel any more emotions than a robot did.

Quinn sat up and watched her dress. Without taking his eyes off her body, he lifted the bottle to his lips and took another swallow.

"That's not the same champagne as you gave me at the gala, is it?" Diana asked quietly.

"It's better," he said. "Have some."

After pulling his shirt back over her shoulders, she took the bottle and sat on the cushion next to him. She stared at the label. "Patricia was right."

He was frowning at her. She could feel it, although she couldn't bring herself to look at him.

"She wasn't even close," Quinn said. "That was her father's stock, not hers, and I doubt they sell that vintage at the Driskill. Don't let her start messing with you."

"She wants to marry you."

The boats bobbed, the water lapping at the edge of their dock. The sun was setting beyond the boathouse door.

Quinn took the bottle out of her hand, so Diana stared at the weathered wood at her bare feet.

"I don't want to marry her. Why are we having this discussion?"

"You should marry her. You will. Her, or someone like her. She'll glide into your life as easily as these boats come in here. You've got a good life, and she'll keep it all so perfect for you."

He made a sound like a hiss, sucking air in quickly, like he'd been punched. Startled, Diana looked at him.

"How can you make love to me and then tell me to marry someone else?"

Because I'm a terrible person.

He stood, a sudden, angry movement. He held the bottle in front of her. "Why did you give me this?"

"It was for Patricia. A hostess gift."

He reared back, actually moved his head back as if

she'd taken a swing at him. Then, in a stiff and formal way, he said, "I misinterpreted it."

He paced a short distance. Two steps away from her. Two steps back. "I misinterpreted it, and you let me. You came here with me, and you let me make love to you. Why?" He gestured toward the cushions. "What was this for you?"

She couldn't answer. Her heart was breaking, because she'd hurt him. This was worse, so much worse, than she'd thought it would be. Her tears weren't blinding enough. She could see the look on Quinn's face. The disbelief. The fury.

When she didn't answer, he repeated his question, louder, his voice echoing off the water and the walls. "What was this for you?"

He walked two steps away from her and stayed away, this time. "Was this some kind of revenge sex? Patricia was mean to you, so you showed her. You had sex with the guy she wants. My God. You accused me of idiotic booty calls. At least shallow sex is honest. But this. What the hell was this?"

"Please, please stop." The tears were falling hard now, and she dashed her cheek on her shoulder, on his shirt.

Quinn stopped, but it cost him physical effort. Breathing hard, like he'd run for miles, he came back to her. "Tell me. What has this whole weekend been about?"

She held up her hands helplessly. "It wasn't about anything. It was just another date. We've been hanging out. We've been buddies. I'm good old Diana, the gal pal, the party girl."

Quinn shoved his hand through his hair. "No, that's wrong. We're dating, because we like being together more than we like being apart. But we're not really together, are we? You only see me when you've taken care of everyone and everything else. Until this morning, I never knew just how important your work with your dogs was. You've shut me out."

She'd kept him at bay for her own protection. Why let the man invade every corner of her life, when they weren't going to be together long?

Quinn turned and chucked the champagne bottle into the nearest trash can, then grabbed his T-shirt off the dock and pulled it on. "I'll tell you what this weekend was supposed to be about. It was about that 'more' that I thought you wanted. It was about including you in my life, my whole life, not just dinners after work. I wanted you to see that you could fit into my world."

Diana felt tears prick her eyes again. He cared about her that much. Or he had cared. "I'm so sorry it backfired. I knew from the first night that no matter how I felt about you, we were too different. I'm not the right woman for you. Now you're finally seeing it."

"No, I'm not." Quinn closed the distance between them, and then to her surprise, he buried his hands in her hair and tilted her face up to his, as if he was going to kiss her. "I see the opposite. The director of Texas Rescue is ready to hire you, if you haven't noticed. Karen is grateful you can handle Patricia, because she can't. You do very well in my world."

If that was true, it was frightening. "Then here's the problem. I don't want to be part of this world. I want to make people happy, not put them in their place. It may sound weak to you, but I would rather leave than fight. I'm leaving."

Quinn was silent for a long time, looking into her eyes. "Then I'm leaving with you."

"Oh." She placed her hands on his wrists. It was so Quinn of him, to insist on escorting a woman home. "I don't mean for the weekend. I mean forever."

"So do I."

Incredibly, he kissed her. Tenderly. Brushing his lips over hers, then over her cheek, then her temple. It didn't feel like a goodbye kiss.

"Quinn, don't you understand what I'm saying?"

"You said you weren't the right woman no matter how you felt about me. What feeling is that? How do you feel about me?"

"It's... I feel..." She wanted him. She liked him, she admired him. He made her laugh, but he also made her angry, and uncomfortable, and—she couldn't put a name to it. She spent so much time telling herself she couldn't have him, she put so much effort into not feeling too much for him, that she couldn't come up with an answer.

With his hands still cupping her face, she shook her head a little, helpless and silent.

"It's okay." He kissed her again, and let her go. "I know how you feel about me. You told me with your body, right here, while we were making love."

She wrapped her arms around her middle, feeling cold without him. Confused. "Revenge sex? I thought that was revenge sex."

Quinn knelt at her feet and held her glittery sandal so she could slip into it. She put her hand on his shoulder for balance, and he looked up at her. The darkness was coming rapidly, but she could tell that he was smiling. *Smiling.*

"You weren't getting revenge on Patricia. That was a bad choice of words. You were showing her, and me, and especially yourself that you own me. That I'm yours for the taking."

When her second sandal was on, he stood and took her hand, lifting it to his lips, a formal cavalier in a T-shirt. "That feeling is right and true. It makes you, and only you, the right woman for me. We're leaving. Together."

When they reached the house, they found Karen on the phone and everyone else packing. The National Weather Service had issued new warnings. The hurricane was not obeying the predictions. It was stronger and faster, and it would hit the coast of Texas before the sun set again.

Everyone left, together.

Chapter Eighteen

Monday morning dawned gray and wet. The hurricane had made landfall hours before, damaging several towns along the coast. Its speed had enabled some of the outer bands of rain to reach as far inland as Austin, but the rain was all that was left of the storm system. As fast as the hurricane had come, it had died once it began moving over land. The Texas Rescue and Relief temporary hospital team was already on their way to the coast. Quinn and Diana were supposed to be on their way, too, to join them sometime before darkness fell.

"I'm running late."

Quinn prayed for patience.

He found it.

"I can wait," he said into the phone. He was in his truck, the pickup he used for everyday driving and disaster relief alike. The plan was to follow Diana's car to the coast. He'd much rather have Diana by his side for the three-hour drive, but policy was policy. Every member of the team was supposed to have their own transportation as well as extra gasoline.

Diana sounded upbeat. "With our separate cars, there's no need for you to be late just because I'm running late. I've got two more errands."

"Any half-ton bags of dog food involved? I'm dressed for it this time." Although he'd be seeing patients on the coast as he did in Austin, he wore jeans and boots, ready for any heavy labor that was needed to get the temporary hospital up and running.

"No, nothing like that. The rain is going to slow down traffic as is. Don't wait for me."

Quinn had never claimed to read people, not the way someone like Diana could. But when it came to Diana herself, Quinn knew her better than anyone else. Her voice came across as too cheerful, too much like she'd been at his mother's picnic.

She was sad.

He drove in the rain to her house, arriving in time to see her lime-green Bug backing out of the driveway. Feeling like the worst kind of stalker, he followed her. Her first errand was to the duplex where she'd left her banana suitcase, which she put in her trunk. Simple. Logical.

Her second was to a cemetery.

Quinn sat in his truck for a long while, watching Diana wind her way between the grave markers, her blue jeans hugging her hips and her pink sequin shirt looking undimmed by the gray weather. He couldn't see her face under the black umbrella she used.

He felt all the inadequacy of their relationship. They'd

taken it up a notch this weekend, it was true. He'd told her she owned him, which she did, and he'd convinced her not to run away despite his alleged friends doing their best to shut her out. But when she hadn't been able to name her emotions, he'd told her it was okay. He hadn't said how he felt about her, either.

It wasn't okay.

I failed to do my best.

And now Diana was alone in a cemetery, unaware how much he cared.

Quinn grabbed his cowboy hat from the rack in his truck cab. The rain had slowed to a drizzle, and the hat's brim kept the worst of it from rolling down his neck as he set off to find Diana.

She was sitting on a plastic tablecloth, umbrella on her shoulder, reading from a white piece of paper. She looked almost like a little girl at a tea party, with the tablecloth underneath her like that.

Quinn stopped at what he gauged to be a respectful distance, but her words reached him as she held the paper up.

"There's enough misery in the world without you adding yours to it. Not you personally, of course. You're a baby. You're allowed to cry. But I really like this philosophy, and I hope you do, too, when you're old enough to decide on your own what to believe in."

The punch to his gut was not going to pass. Quinn didn't even try to wait it out. He walked through the wet grass.

She saw him coming and stopped reading. She looked at her letter, and she looked at him, and she looked so confused, Quinn knew she'd never been interrupted before. She moved to get to her feet, but he was there first. "Don't get up. May I sit down?"

"You're not supposed to be here."

"I know."

"Did you follow me?"

"Yes."

He didn't sit beside her, but took a knee instead, keeping his boot off the tablecloth. He removed his hat and held it over his heart, as his parents had taught him since his youngest days.

"May I?" he said, as he took the handle of her umbrella and held it over them both.

He wondered how many years Diana's mother had had to teach her daughter all the ways of the world. He looked at the date on the tombstone. The first punch hadn't lessened yet, or he surely would have felt a second.

"Diana." His voice was raw, little more than a whisper. He cleared his throat. "What year were you born?"

She sighed and put the paper in her lap. Her letter, her precious letter.

"She died the day after I was born. There was some complication with the pregnancy, and they told her she'd have to stay in the hospital for the last four weeks before I was due. On the second day, she wrote my letter."

Diana affected a slightly different voice, the one she must have imagined her mother used. "It's so incredibly boring here. I think I'll use the news hour to write you a letter every day. I'll pick one topic, and try to tell you what I know. That will be so much better than an hour of doom and gloom on this hospital TV."

Diana looked down at the letter in her hand. Not the

original letter, Quinn realized, but a photocopy, much folded.

Diana talked in her usual voice. "In the first letter, she wrote about happiness. The next day, she suffered a stroke or an aneurysm or something. My grandpa just called it 'an attack.' She never regained consciousness. I was born by C-section two weeks later, and they took her off life support."

"Good God." He bowed his head.

She was quiet until he opened his eyes again. "You're a doctor. Don't you see things like this all the time?"

He hoped his voice wouldn't fail him. "No. Those cases are rare. You can't help but feel the loss."

"Don't start crying, okay? It will make me cry."

"Okay." Quinn cleared his throat again.

After a moment of silence, Diana looked at him out of the corner of her eye, as if she were shy. "But you do think some of the doctors might have cried when she passed away? Maybe a little?"

"I know they did."

These punches were killing him. The hair on the back of his neck practically stood up, so strongly did he feel that he was seeing a glimpse of a very young child in Diana's shy question.

By the time she'd been old enough to ask about her mother, those who'd known her would have had years to adjust to her mother's passing. Diana had probably been told the story in the same straightforward way she'd just told it to Quinn. All of her questions through the years must have been answered matter-of-factly.

It must have seemed to her as if no one mourned her mother. Maybe it still seemed that way to her.

"I guarantee you that when Leslie Diana Connor died,

all the nurses wept. And when the ones who hadn't been on duty came to work later that day, they wept, too, when they saw a new patient in her bed. Every doctor had to take a few moments to step into an office or a bathroom or a broom closet so that they could get themselves together before calling on their next patient. Your grandfather was torn up, so much so that he still found it hard to talk about years later, so he probably didn't talk about it much at all. But everyone—every single person, Diana—everyone wished they could have saved your mother for you."

He couldn't look at her. The tombstone in front of him was a wet blur, and if he looked at Diana, he would surely cry when she'd asked him not to.

"Thank you," she said, breathless. "That was the best story, ever."

He ditched the umbrella and hauled her to her feet and pulled her into his arms. She was crying, and she squeezed him back as tightly as he was hugging her.

"Thank you," she repeated, "thank you, thank you."

"Yeah," he said, and he kissed her soft hair and her wet cheeks, then held her a little longer as he read the tombstone once more. "Happy birthday."

Diana couldn't cry anymore, not here, not in what was left of this coastal town.

It was her birthday, and all around her, everywhere she looked, people were devastated. Their houses were gone. Their shops, their roads, their lives, all damaged. They kept coming to the medical tents, carrying their belongings in a suitcase or pillowcase, wearing clothes that were tailored or torn, signing in, asking for help.

Diana couldn't help.

Blood made her faint.

She hadn't known this. She'd never been around blood before, or at least, not around this kind of blood. This wasn't a scraped knee or a finger-prick kind of blood, but the kind that caked around a broken bone that poked through the skin. That made her faint.

When she fainted, she made everyone's jobs harder. On this birthday, she'd been labeled a fainter, and had become a burden to the hospital. Not to the town's real hospital, with its shattered windows and the roof that had been peeled back and ripped halfway off. Not that hospital, but the one housed in white tents that had been set up in its shadow. The one Texas Rescue ran. The one where Quinn worked, and Patricia, and Karen, and everyone except Diana, because she was a fainter.

There's enough misery in the world without you adding yours to it.

Diana wouldn't cry, not when everyone had a better reason to be sad than she did.

Patricia would show her no mercy if she cried. While Diana had been alphabetizing the medicine, a little boy had been wheeled past her as he spit blood from his broken teeth and then proudly, gleefully, viciously smiled at every adult he passed. Diana had felt light-headed for one second, and then she'd been on the floor with little plastic pill bottles raining down on her.

The alphabetizing had begun again without her. Patricia, disgusted Patricia, had sent her to the X-ray tent to hand clipboards and paperwork to waiting patients. That had lasted less than five minutes. Diana had cracked her elbow hard on her way down during that faint, and her shirt had caught on something that pulled the right thread to cause a line of pink sequins to start falling off, one by one. She'd insisted her elbow would be okay, but still, she'd been almost grateful to be kicked out of the X-ray tent.

So, she was spending the rest of her birthday in the parking lot, in a chair, sitting in a tent with its flaps down. She was sweltering, but no one wanted to risk having the new girl catch a glimpse of any gory injuries among the people who waited in the line for medical attention. She kept track of the walkie-talkies. Local cellphone towers had been knocked out, so the hospital ran on battery-operated handheld devices. When someone came to change out their battery, Diana wrote down the serial number on a clipboard.

In other words, the hospital ran just fine without her.

Diana sat alone, hour after hour, and felt the full weight of her uselessness.

The one touchstone in her life, her mother's letter, seemed frivolous in the face of all this disaster. *Find moments of beauty.* Where? Light and reflection and sparkle meant nothing here, nothing. Ice was used for injuries, not to fill tubs of drinks for friends. Candles were used as an inferior source of light when batteries died. Dogs were used to find corpses in collapsed buildings.

Where was the happiness?

The flap of the tent opened behind her, and Quinn walked in.

She turned, took one look at his face, and knew she wasn't the only one having a bad day.

Chapter Nineteen

Quinn had left the main treatment tent with a mental list of things he needed. He needed to find Patricia, so that she could light a fire under someone to source more nitroglycerin. He needed the second generator fixed, because they could only keep one set of equipment charged without it. He needed better lighting, now that the sun was going down. He needed a fresh battery for his two-way radio.

When he lifted the white flap and saw Diana with her whiskey-colored hair, every other need became secondary.

She walked straight to him, and gave him a hug.

Damn. It was still a little alarming, the way she did that, but it was exactly what he needed. He slid his stethoscope off his neck and tossed it on the table, then wrapped both arms securely around her. She leaned into him, so he could lean into her, too, and they stayed that way, taking some of the weight off each other.

Quinn closed his eyes.

In the wake of any natural disaster, an unfortunate spike in the amount of heart attacks occurred in any community. Quinn could deal with that. It was why he was here. Most MIs required stabilizing medicines and transportation to the nearest city whose hospital was still in working order. Today, two patients had needed more.

Quinn had performed CPR on the first patient, applying the hard and deep compressions with the heels of his hands and the force of his entire upper body, while the team had scrambled to find the portable defibrillator in a room not yet completely ready. It had taken a long, long time, an eternity, and Quinn would feel the effort tomorrow in his triceps, he knew, but the patient had survived.

It wasn't the first time he'd had a human's life in his hands—literally, under his hands—as he forced a heart to pump. It wouldn't be the last. But it wasn't a normal part of his routine; he was an interventional cardiologist, not an emergency physician.

Diana felt so good in his tired arms.

The second patient had died. Quinn had thought of Diana's mother, and he'd thought about the way he was leaving too much unsaid with her daughter.

Quinn started to let go, but Diana held him tightly. He put his arms back around her. She owned him. If she needed him, then she could have him.

"Is this for you, for me, or for us?" he asked quietly.

"I think we've both had a hard day."

She kept her cheek pressed against him. He brushed

her hair back with his hand. "You do know there is an 'us,' right?"

She frowned, a tiny movement of her brow. "Yes, of course."

"In the boathouse, when I said you owned me—"

"We're exclusive. We're dating."

"No." He ran his thumb over her cheekbone. "No, there's more to us than that. I love you, Diana."

She picked her head up and looked at him, just looked at him, for the longest moment. She was beautiful. Quinn wanted to look at her forever. He planned on looking at her, forever.

"I can't think of anyone who deserves to be loved more than you, Diana. I don't think you've had enough of it in your life."

"I deserve it?" she asked. "Everyone deserves to be loved. I'm nothing special."

"You are extraordinary."

She looked down, fingering the edge of her sequined shirt, his compliment making her shy.

"Please, let me go," she said.

Something was bothering her. He relaxed his hold so she could slip out, but her next words froze his heart.

"Let me go this time, when I leave. I'm not the right woman for you."

She wasn't shy. She just didn't love him.

Every crack he'd felt in his heart, every hint of ice, came at him at once, a barrage of freezing shards.

"I'm so sorry," she whispered, and she took a step backward.

He worked hard to push through that first punch. This didn't make sense. He knew this woman. He knew her. She had strong feelings about him.

"You're sorry for what?" he asked.

"I'm sorry I let you talk me into staying every time I tried to leave. I shouldn't have been your lover, not when I knew we weren't a match."

"Not a match." He recaptured her, and pulled her tightly to him, so her jean-clad legs brushed against his. "That's a lie."

The tent flap opened and a man walked in. Diana pushed away from Quinn and stood at a little distance, crossing her arms over her chest.

The man held up the battery for his radio and gestured toward the storage rack. "So, I'll just…uh. Right." He grabbed a new battery and left.

The tent was stifling. Quinn didn't know how she'd stood it all day. "Come take a walk with me."

He pushed aside the back flap so they'd avoid the busiest part of the tent city. The edge of the parking lot bordered a drainage ditch. It was nearly overflowing, full from the hurricane's downfall, but the water was moving, draining, slowly returning to normal. The coming twilight promised some respite from the heat.

Diana stepped up onto a concrete parking barrier, fidgeting rather than facing him.

Quinn hoped she was listening. "I respect your matchmaking intuition, more than you do. Think about that very first night. The very first moment you saw me, you noticed me, didn't you? Every instinct inside you must have sent you toward me. You wanted to be my friend. You wanted me to be happy, from the first minute we met."

"I try to cheer people up all the time." She stepped off the barrier and put her hands into her front pockets.

"I left you at the gala. After I found you a good match, I walked away."

"And I came after you."

"You shouldn't have."

"I've got instincts, too, and every one told me to hold on to you. *Don't let this one go*. We belong together, Diana." He reached for her arm and ran his fingers from her elbow to her wrist, so that she removed her hand from her pocket. They faced each other, so close, but touching only those two hands.

After a long moment, she took her other hand out of her pocket and placed it over his. "This is so hard to say, but Quinn, we have no future together. Don't you see? You're thinking with your heart, but I'm being realistic. I know the limits of my matchmaking skills. I've seen so many first loves turn sour. Do you remember Stewy's mom? I think her new boyfriend is right for her, but I thought that six months ago, too, with a different guy, and I was wrong. The animal shelter is full of sad endings. It's frightening, when you see someone leave with a new puppy, so very happy, and they come back in a few months or a year, convinced that it's impossible to live with that dog one more day."

She was so tenderhearted, Quinn had no doubt that she felt the pain of every abandoned dog. "I'm in love with you, Diana. That's not going to change."

"We're like…we're like a Yorkie and a rancher. It doesn't matter how much the rancher is taken with the Yorkie. It doesn't matter if he thinks the puppy is cute and fun. If he takes that Yorkie home, he's still not going to have the help he needs to bring the horses in from the pasture, is he? It's not a good match. He may keep that dog until the day he dies, just like you might keep me around, but they won't live the happy lives they could have had, because they were paired up with the wrong partner."

She dropped his hand only to press her palms flat on the muscle of his chest. She rose on her toes the tiniest bit, and she kissed him gently, beautifully on the mouth.

She stepped back. "I won't do that to you, Quinn. Goodbye."

Diana tried to find the beauty in the heartbreak. She took another step back. The sunset was spectacular. The water edging the asphalt looked like a silver pond.

Quinn MacDowell looked furious. *"Don't you ever kiss me like that again."*

Diana started walking in the general direction of the farthest corner of the parking lot, where the Texas Rescue personnel had parked their vehicles.

Quinn followed, his boots loud as they struck the asphalt. "You're really going to walk away, aren't you? You're going to live the rest of your life as a martyr. You're going to tell yourself you did the right thing, the noble thing, and let me go on to find someone more suitable."

It was exactly what she'd had in mind. She walked faster. "Don't make this more difficult than it already is."

"Difficult? You want to know what difficult is? It's being crazy in love with a woman, and hearing what a low opinion she has of herself. Your Yorkie analogy sucks."

Diana flinched a little at the way the word *sucks* ricocheted off the asphalt. The parking lot for the damaged hospital building was huge, like a shopping mall's. They had acres to go.

"You're not a dog, damn it. You are a human being

with the power to change, the power to affect the world around her, the power to make her life anything she wants it to be. That Yorkie crap is a cop-out. It gives you the excuse to never change. It's easy to say, 'This is how I was born, this is how I have to stay.'"

She wished he would be quiet. He was ruining her moment. Her heart hurt because she had to leave him, but she couldn't give in to the pain, because Quinn was right beside her, and he wouldn't shut up.

"Let's try your analogy with humans in it. If you decided to live with the rancher, then you could become one, too. If he needed help bringing the horses in from pasture, you could learn how to do it. If you didn't enjoy it, you could say, 'Hey, honey, let's hire a ranch hand to do this.' There's an option your Yorkie didn't have.

"Your little analogy doesn't address the real problem. You're not selfish enough. You're so busy trying to make sure everyone else is happy, you forget to go after what you want. You give away your home and your car and your time and your talents. You would rather leave than fight for something that you want, just so someone else won't be unhappy for even a moment."

And that was the last straw. Diana stopped walking and rounded on Quinn.

"It's good to make other people happy. It's bad to make them miserable. That's what my mother said." Quinn had seen her letter at the start of this endless, horrible day, and now he was insulting it. Her mother's letter.

She hated the tears that pricked her eyes.

Quinn spoke with a little less heat. "I know, and she was right. It's noble and honorable to wish nothing but happiness for those around you, and you do. But when it comes to your happiness, you have to be greedy. This is your life, and if you want to be happy, then you might have to demand it for yourself. Start small. If your talents aren't being used in an asinine walkie-talkie tent, then go find yourself a position you'll enjoy."

"You're asking me to throw away every philosophy I've built my life on."

"No. Your mother's letter says it takes courage to be happy. Maybe she didn't mean the courage to try bungee jumping or to go solo to a ball. Maybe she wanted you to have the courage to take what you want. I can love you, Diana. But you've got to get greedy. You've got to keep me for yourself."

Be greedy. Be selfish. And then, she'd become happy? It went against everything she knew.

"You have choices to make," Quinn said, and he sounded kind. "So do I. I choose not to stand here and watch you drive off into the sunset. It won't make me happy."

Quinn turned and started the long trek back to the hospital. Diana watched him go.

Then she walked slowly the rest of the way to her car, curled up in the backseat, and read her mother's letter until it was too dark to see.

If the backseat of her car couldn't hold a Saint Bernard, then Diana had been foolish to think it could hold her. By the time dawn sent rays of light through her car window, she ached in every muscle. Dragging her banana suitcase behind her, she returned to the hospital.

Feeling a million times better after brushing her teeth and changing her clothes, she went to find Patricia in the administration tent.

Quinn had said it would be starting small, but it felt like a big step as she faced Patricia over a collapsible conference table.

"I need a different assignment."

Patricia didn't glance up. "You're not qualified to do anything except clerical work, and those spots are filled right now with people who do not pass out at the sight of blood."

Patricia's workstation was in a tent with a generator and an air cooler, Diana noted. But Patricia worked hard, there was no denying it.

"There must be something I can do to help," Diana said.

"Look, you may think I'm being a bitch, but I'm not. I've got responsibilities. When you passed out in the X-ray tent, the techs told me you missed cracking your head on the corner of the table by a fraction of an inch. I don't knowingly put volunteers in harm's way. It isn't how I operate."

"I'm glad to hear it," Diana said mildly. She doubted she'd ever be friends with Patricia, but she could still think of her as a Dalmatian, particularly when Patricia tilted her head just the right way.

Patricia stood and picked up her two-way radio and her notebook. "I don't have time to find a new spot for you. Keep yourself busy today or go home, I don't care."

She left her usual uncomfortable silence in her wake, as the other volunteers in the tent stayed busy. Diana turned to the friendliest-looking one. "Are there any dogs around here?"

The woman shook her head. "No, but we've got kids out the wazoo."

"Are they bleeding? Not that I wouldn't want to help, but I kind of go 'timber' when I get around that stuff."

The woman laughed. "Oh, I heard about you yesterday. No, the recovery ward should have them all nicely bandaged up. Here, I'll show you which tent it is."

The only way to tell the area was pediatric was that the patients were children. Otherwise, it was all white walls and white bed linens. The patients had white bandages, but there was no blood. A few had IV needles, but that didn't bother Diana in the least.

Parents were attempting to entertain the kids with varying degrees of success. Portable electronic devices had died. Card games seemed to be more successful, but there was a shortage of games. There was a shortage of everything.

Most especially, there was a shortage of happiness.

"I was thinking of having a party," Diana said casually, when she noticed a few children looking at her as she stood in the door. "What kind of party do you think we should have?"

The news started filtering into the adult treatment area around eleven o'clock.

More nitroglycerin had been located, purchased, transported and stocked in the pharmacy, and the nicest young woman had taken over the pediatric recovery area.

Everything she did was described as darling. She herself was darling. The sock puppets she'd made for the kids were just darling. She was also generous, clever and creative. Long before Quinn heard the first male gossip, that she was the hot chick who'd fainted twice yesterday, he'd already known the darling they were talking about was his.

He hoped.

It was nearly three before he could escape to the pediatric recovery ward.

Quinn stood in the doorway and took in the scene. Where yesterday there had been fear and worry, today there were sock puppets. Dozens and dozens of them, one for each hand of the children in beds and the children running around. Some for the parents to use, so their puppets could talk to their children's puppets.

The eyes were made of plastic gems, and their bodies were made from the material of various pieces of Diana's wardrobe. Quinn recognized the sequined cherries. She must have run out of socks and started cutting up her shirts to keep the supply of puppets going.

He saw her before she saw him. She was leaning against a bed, using one of the curved needles from surgery to sew her next creation, and she was beautiful. Her shirt was plain white with no gems remaining on it, but she was still dazzling, full-color Diana.

She looked good in pure white. The last bachelor MacDowell didn't find the thought frightening at all.

"Hey, mister. Are you going to listen to my heart?"

Quinn looked down at the young boy who was pointing at the stethoscope around his neck. "Not today."

"Are you here for the party?"

Quinn kept his eyes on Diana, waiting for her to look at him. Just one look, and he'd know if this new venture meant she'd decided to be selfish about him as well as her job.

She looked. She smiled. And she bounced on her toes, just a little bit.

Quinn walked straight to her and gave her a hug.

She clung to him, hard, and he could feel her laughing in his arms. Or crying. Or both.

The boy had trailed him across the room. "So didja come for the party?"

"Yes. I'm here to get my party on."

"Oh, it's not just a party," Diana said. "It's a dog party."

A dozen little puppets started barking, their high-pitched operators making little "arf, arf" noises. Quinn raised an eyebrow at Diana, who was wincing. "You find this worse than the real barking at your shelter?"

"A hundred times worse. And it was my idea." She picked up a tube sewn out of cherry-sequined material. "Stick out your hand. Can you tell what kind of dog it is?"

Quinn couldn't hazard a guess.

She wriggled it onto his hand differently, and tufted up some strips of material in the center of its head.

"It's a Yorkie. They're super cute, and I hear guys who own real ranches really like them."

Then Diana murmured in his ear, "But I'm much, much better to have around. I love you like crazy, Quinn MacDowell, and I'm gonna make you one happy man."

Epilogue

Quinn had the whole family in on the secret.

Diana thought he was still working on the coast with Texas Rescue, but he'd been home for two hours now. Two hours that he'd spent having not enough time to set up the party and too much time to second-guess his sanity.

Diana's real birthday had been Monday. She'd told him she loved him on Tuesday—thank God. She'd left with only the de-jeweled clothing on her back later that night, because she'd had to go back to work here in Austin. Today was Saturday, and Quinn had decided that a mere five days wasn't too late to throw her a birthday party.

The part of the equation that made him question his sanity was this: he'd met Diana four weeks ago. Four weeks and one day. Was it too soon to propose?

Jamie, who'd eloped after knowing Kendry for four weeks, had said the timing was irrelevant. Braden had too wisely pointed out that only Diana could decide if it was too soon. Both brothers had given him their blessing to offer Diana their grandmother's engagement ring. They'd chosen different rings for their brides, each for special reasons.

Quinn hoped the girl who valued everything she'd been handed down from her mother would value the ring from his father's mother.

She would. Of course she would. She'd say yes.

Quinn cleared his throat and looked out the front window of Diana's house—the blue one—and waited for the lime-green Bug to make its appearance.

In the end, the surprise went off without a hitch. Diana was thrilled with his mother's cake, Lana and Kendry had managed to buy her gifts in her size, a feat Quinn wasn't certain how women accomplished, and both of his brothers had covered for him when he'd gone outside to add the finishing touch to his proposal.

"Come out in the sunshine with me," he said, taking Diana's hand to give her a boost out of the armchair. She looked like sunshine herself in a bright yellow sundress. Quinn wished he'd changed from his jeans and blue shirt, suddenly. He should have worn a suit and tie for the occasion.

As soon as they were out of his mother's line of sight, Diana whispered in his ear. "Have I told you how delicious you look? I love you in blue."

Quinn decided he should stop trying to figure out how she knew what he needed to hear.

And then they were outside, and the sky was blue,

the grass was green, and the whole world consisted of only the two of them.

She immediately noticed the clothesline he'd strung up, of course. From it fluttered a dozen homemade children's cards with a dozen childish variations on the spelling of "Happy Birthday."

"When did they make these?" she asked, going down the line and touching each one.

"The day after you left. Crayons arrived in a Red Cross package."

She stepped back to take in the whole clothesline. He watched her profile as she nodded, just once, in approval.

"It looks very happy," she said.

"It looks like you. This is what you bring to my world, Diana. This is what you bring to everyone's world, but I'm selfish enough to want you by my side at the end of every day. I've missed you this week. Four days without sunshine felt more like four weeks."

"Four years."

He got down on one knee and revealed the gray velvet box he'd been keeping in his hand. The speech he'd so carefully prepared flew out of his mind, so he said what seemed right for the moment. "Will you please marry me? Will you please bring dogs into my home and chaos into my life? I love you, Diana. You're color and sunshine and everything good in the world. You're my happiness."

Diana nodded and nodded, then began fluttering her hands in front of her cheeks and blinking her eyelashes. "Oh," she choked out. "I don't want to cry."

"I don't, either. Please say yes."

"Yes! Oh, yes, of course. I'm sorry, I didn't think. I couldn't talk, and—"

Quinn stood and kissed her swiftly on the mouth. A round of applause came from the side of the house—so much for privacy—and his family joined them with crystal champagne flutes as they toasted the good life, with the good stuff.

* * * * *

COMING NEXT MONTH FROM

HARLEQUIN

SPECIAL EDITION

Available May 20, 2014

#2335 FORTUNE'S PRINCE
The Fortunes of Texas: Welcome to Horseback Hollow
by Allison Leigh
A beautiful British royal, Amelia Fortune Chesterfield has traveled the globe, but she's never met anyone quite like cowboy Quinn Drummond. After one passionate night with Quinn, Amelia finds herself pregnant and uncertain about her future. Will the ravishing royal create a forever family with the rugged rancher, or are they fated to remain apart?

#2336 DESTINY'S LAST BACHELOR?
Welcome to Destiny • by Christyne Butler
Hollywood starlet Priscilla Lennon decides to dodge the paparazzi by fleeing to Destiny, Wyoming. There she meets down-and-out East Coaster Dean Zippenella, who's smitten with the sultry stranger. It's a case of Hollywood meets the Jersey Shore, but can Dean and Priscilla meet in the middle to find true love?

#2337 THE SINGLE DAD'S SECOND CHANCE
Those Engaging Garretts! • by Brenda Harlen
It's Valentine's Day, and dateless Rachel Ellis plans to work through it at her flower shop...until Andrew Garrett comes along. The sexy single dad worries how dating might affect his daughter, Maura, but Rachel's not just any woman. In fact, good-looking Garrett might find his future coming up roses....

#2338 TO CATCH A CAMDEN
The Camdens of Colorado • by Victoria Pade
After a bad divorce, botanist Gia Grant is staying focused on studying plants...*not* handsome bad boys like Derek Camden. Derek wants to pay back Gia's neighbors for a bad turn his grandfather did them years ago, and he needs Gia's help to complete his mission. But disdain might blossom into love sooner than Gia thinks!

#2339 THE BABY TRUTH
Men of the West • by Stella Bagwell
A double whammy just hit Sassy Matthews—she just found out that she's adopted *and* she's pregnant with her now-deceased ex's baby. Sassy's determined to make a home for her child and find her own roots. When she meets lawyer-rancher Jett Sundell, their attraction is electric, but is he the man who can give her the family she's always wanted?

#2340 A BREVIA BEGINNING
by Michelle Major
U.S. marshal Scott Callahan is looking to turn over a new leaf in life, so he moves to Brevia, North Carolina, where he impulsively buys a local bar. Lawyer Lexi Preston's got it even worse—she just got fired *and* she is the town pariah. To get by, she goes to work at Scott's bar. Lexi might just be the worst server ever, but she's got a knack for finding her perfect man....

YOU CAN FIND MORE INFORMATION ON UPCOMING HARLEQUIN® TITLES, FREE EXCERPTS AND MORE AT WWW.HARLEQUIN.COM.

HSECNM0514

REQUEST YOUR FREE BOOKS!
2 FREE NOVELS PLUS 2 FREE GIFTS!

⊕HARLEQUIN°

SPECIAL EDITION
Life, Love & Family

YES! Please send me 2 FREE Harlequin® Special Edition novels and my 2 FREE gifts (gifts are worth about $10). After receiving them, if I don't wish to receive any more books, I can return the shipping statement marked "cancel." If I don't cancel, I will receive 6 brand-new novels every month and be billed just $4.74 per book in the U.S. or $5.24 per book in Canada. That's a savings of at least 14% off the cover price! It's quite a bargain! Shipping and handling is just 50¢ per book in the U.S. and 75¢ per book in Canada.* I understand that accepting the 2 free books and gifts places me under no obligation to buy anything. I can always return a shipment and cancel at any time. Even if I never buy another book, the two free books and gifts are mine to keep forever.

235/335 HDN F45Y

Name _____ (PLEASE PRINT) _____

Address _____ Apt. # _____

City _____ State/Prov. _____ Zip/Postal Code _____

Signature (if under 18, a parent or guardian must sign) _____

Mail to the **Harlequin® Reader Service:**
IN U.S.A.: P.O. Box 1867, Buffalo, NY 14240-1867
IN CANADA: P.O. Box 609, Fort Erie, Ontario L2A 5X3

Want to try two free books from another line?
Call 1-800-873-8635 or visit www.ReaderService.com.

* Terms and prices subject to change without notice. Prices do not include applicable taxes. Sales tax applicable in N.Y. Canadian residents will be charged applicable taxes. Offer not valid in Quebec. This offer is limited to one order per household. Not valid for current subscribers to Harlequin Special Edition books. All orders subject to credit approval. Credit or debit balances in a customer's account(s) may be offset by any other outstanding balance owed by or to the customer. Please allow 4 to 6 weeks for delivery. Offer available while quantities last.

Your Privacy—The Harlequin® Reader Service is committed to protecting your privacy. Our Privacy Policy is available online at www.ReaderService.com or upon request from the Harlequin Reader Service.

We make a portion of our mailing list available to reputable third parties that offer products we believe may interest you. If you prefer that we not exchange your name with third parties, or if you wish to clarify or modify your communication preferences, please visit us at www.ReaderService.com/consumerchoice or write to us at Harlequin Reader Service Preference Service, P.O. Box 9062, Buffalo, NY 14269. Include your complete name and address.

HSE13R

Quinn Drummond can't believe blue-blooded beauty Amelia Fortune is back in Horseback Hollow. She'd left him high and dry after their one night of passion months before! But Amelia has returned to the tiny Texas town with a secret—one that might unite the rancher and the royal forever...

***

She turned on the heel of her little sandals, her hair flying around her shoulders, and started walking away, her sweet hips swaying.

He cussed like he hadn't cussed since he was fifteen and his mom had washed out his mouth with soap. "You're not going anywhere, princess." In two long steps, he reached her and hooked her around the waist, swinging her off her feet before she had a chance to stop him.

Her legs scissored, and he slid her over his shoulder, clamping his arm over the back of her legs before she could do either one of them physical damage. "Cut it out."

She drummed her fists against his backside, trying to wriggle out of his hold. "Put me *down* this instant," she ordered imperiously.

"I warned you," he said and swatted her butt.

She pounded his back even harder. "You...cretin."

"Yeah, yeah. Sweet nothings won't get you anywhere, princess." He stomped back into the house and into the living room. He lifted her off his shoulder and dumped her on the sofa.

She bounced and tried scrambling away, but he leaned over her, pinning her on either side with his hands. "Stay," he bit out.

She glared at him through the hair hanging in her face. "I. Don't. Take. Orders." Her chest heaved.

He didn't move.

Didn't do a damn thing even though he should have, because she was there, in his house, and she was pregnant with his kid and he didn't want to ask for a polite dance or gentle, moonlit kisses.

He just *wanted*.

With a need that was blinding.

***

HARLEQUIN®

SPECIAL EDITION

Life, Love and Family

Coming in June 2014 from
Brenda Harlen
THE SINGLE DAD'S SECOND CHANCE

From the reader-favorite miniseries,
Those Engaging Garretts!

It's Valentine's Day, and dateless Rachel Ellis plans
to work through it at her flower shop...until
Andrew Garrett comes along. The sexy single dad
worries how dating might affect his daughter,
Maura, but Rachel's not just any woman. In fact,
good-looking Garrett might find his future coming
up roses....

Already available from
***Those Engaging Garretts!** by Brenda Harlen:*

A VERY SPECIAL DELIVERY
HIS LONG-LOST FAMILY
FROM NEIGHBORS...TO NEWLYWEDS?

www.Harlequin.com

HSE65819